A

Rose

Among

Thorns

II

Jimmy DaSaint

A ROSE AMONG THORNS II

Published by DASAINT ENTERTAINMENT
Po Box 97 Bala Cynwyd, PA 19004
Website: www.dasaintentertainment.com

THE CIRCLE OF ETERNAL LOVE

The circle of eternal love
Is a circle that can never be broken
It protects love from all outside intruders
It will overcome all obstacles
And persevere through all adversity
The circle of eternal love is timeless, endless and
unbreakable
It cannot be moved, shattered or blemished
No harm will ever penetrate it

-Jimmy DaSaint

Every woman is a rose, waiting to be picked, cherished and appreciated.

-Jimmy DaSaint

Chapter One
A ROSE AMONG THORNS II

Southwest Philly
September 4ᵗʰ...

Eric pulled up in front of his beautiful four-bedroom home and parked his new Mercedes. The street was dark and tranquil and not a soul was outside. As he rolled down the tinted window, he inhaled the calm fall air in through his nostrils. The soulful lyrics of Mary J. Blige flowed from his radio, and Eric sat lost in deep thought.

He reminisced on the past year and a half of his life. He was shot twice, and almost lost his life and his lovely fiancée, Rose. His mind was in constant reflection. He had lost his best friend, Mike, and tearfully watched as the cold, lonely soil swallowed up his casket. Not to mention that he had seen Larry die after Braheem sliced his throat with a razor-sharp switchblade. Eric's mind was full as he thought of it all. Thinking about the gains and the many losses of his young life, he wiped a lonely tear from his eye and rolled up the tinted window. He knew those painful memories would never fade away.

After the song had ended Eric turned off the car's engine and got out. Then he walked towards his house and went inside. Each night he entered his home he was greeted with peace and quiet; and by the pleasant scents from the large scented candles that often filled the air.

After removing his jacket and hanging it up; he took off his Air Nikes and quietly tip-toed up the carpeted stairs. When Eric entered the bedroom, Rose was lying under the covers asleep ever so peacefully, and the sound of her light snoring brought a big smile to his face. Eric picked up her college textbooks from off the bed and sat them on the dresser.

Every day Rose studied hard to receive her degree in Business Management. She had to be extremely focused because she was the manager at two of the daycares that Eric owned; which she ran extraordinarily well. However; after work there was not much time for her to do anything else but to hit the books.

Eric removed his clothes and went into the bathroom to take a long, comforting shower. The warm water felt like soft therapeutic raindrops as they fell down onto his body. The shower was what he needed to help put his mind and body at ease.

After drying himself off, Eric wrapped the thick white towel around his waist and walked back into the bedroom. When he entered the bedroom, Rose was sitting up on the king-sized bed with her arms crossed. She was all smiles as Eric removed his towel and joined Rose in the bed.

"Oh, so you didn't want me to take a shower with you tonight," Rose said.

"No, that's not it. You were sleeping so peacefully and I didn't want to wake you up," Eric said, laying his head back on one of the pillows.

"How was your day," Eric asked.

"Not bad at all. I did well on my test today and after school I went and checked on both of the daycare centers. Everything is going well and my little boyfriend, Billy, he drew me a very nice picture," Rose said, as her smile enlarged as she thought of how cute the gesture was.

"I'mma have to have a nice long talk with Billy," Eric said jokingly.

"He's only five years old boy, plus you know how little boys are. I might be his first crush," Rose said, laying her head on Eric's chest.

"So, baby, how was your day," she asked.

"I was out with Braheem all morning trying to convince him to go back home to his woman."

"Joyce called me earlier today. She's going crazy without Braheem at home," Rose said.

"I told her that she can't force a man to do what she wants; especially a man like Braheem who plays by his own rules. Her jealousy drives him crazy and as long as Joyce keeps acting that way, Braheem will keep packing up his clothes and leaving her," she continued.

"Well, I told him to at least call her. It's been three days since they last talked and I'm tired of Joyce constantly paging me looking for him," Eric said.

"What did Braheem say?"

"He said that he'll call her in a few days, that he needs at least five days away from her to clear his head," Eric laughed.

"You better not ever leave me like that," Rose sat up and said.

"If Billy keeps drawing you pictures, I'mma leave you for a whole week," Eric joked.

Rose playfully pushed his shoulder. "I wrote you a poem today," Rose said, reaching under her

8

pillow and taking out a small notepad. Eric crossed his arms and waited. Rose looked deep into Eric's eyes and smiled. She loved writing him poetry and Eric enjoyed hearing her read her poems.

"What is this one called," he asked.

"It's called *Black Love,* and it's dedicated to you," Rose said.

"I read it to Joyce earlier and she loves it."

"Okay, let me hear it," Eric said anxiously.

"Okay, it goes like this..."

Black love is the most powerful force on earth
Nothing in life can compare
When the love is real and genuine
Everything becomes so clear
When Black Love is at its peak
It's unconditional and pure
We crave for Black Love like an addiction
Yearning for it more and more
The feeling is so much better than sex
The sensation is one of a kind
It's a feeling of unlimited satisfaction
With orgasms that explode in our minds
When you find a Black Love who makes you feel this
way
Never let them go
Because Black Love comes seldom
and for many it's a love they will never know
So if you are one of the lucky ones
Then I'm sure you already know
To always keep your Black Love near
and to never ever let it go

After reading the poem Rose sat the notepad on the nightstand. "Did you like it," she said. "Loved it," Eric said, smiling as he pulled Rose into his strong arms. "And now you're about to find out just how much," Eric said, leaning over and turning off the lamp on the nightstand.

Inside the tranquility of their bedroom, Eric and Rose began making love like two lost lovers who hadn't seen each other in years.

Chapter Two
A ROSE AMONG THORNS II

Inside The Platinum Club...

Tony Perotta, Jr. sat inside his office all alone; staring at a large colorful portrait of his late father which had him consumed with pain and sorrow. While Tony, Jr. was locked away upstate and serving time, his father, and three cousins- Vinny, Mario and Bunny- had all been murdered. Even his godfather, Marty, had been savagely gunned down by two masked men who broke in the club and robbed them for two million dollars.

Tony, Jr. was his parents' only child and now with his father dead Tony, Jr. was the new owner of the well-known Platinum Club. The violent young boss was not only into the night-club business but he was the leader of a gang of wild, young street thugs.

He was known to be a cold-blooded, ruthless killer, and at just twenty-eight years of age he had six bodies under his belt; four of which he committed by using his powerful bare hands. Tony, Jr. stood 6' 4, and weighed close to 250 pounds. He had been a bully all of his life and only his father could control his fiery temper and violent conduct. But now his mentor was no longer around to keep him in check, and there would be no one to control the rage he felt inside.

After Tony, Jr. finished counting $75,000 in cash, he stashed it all inside the hidden wall safe behind his father's oversized portrait. Over one million dollars was neatly stacked inside, and two of his most loyal bodyguards stood outside the door as he handled his fortune.

A sudden knock at the door startled him and Tony quickly locked the safe, placed the portrait back in front of it, and sat down at his desk. "Come in," he said. One of his bodyguards stuck his head in and said, "Boss, its Heaven. She's dressed and ready to talk to you." Tony replied, "Send her in."

As he took out a Newport and lit it up, Heaven walked into the large office and shut the door behind her. Tony looked at Heaven's beautiful face, smooth dark complexion, and tall model-like body as he smiled. Heaven was The Platinum Club's number one exotic dancer. After Bunny was murdered and Rose quit, Heaven took over the lucrative position.

Gloria "Heaven" Jones was a twenty-six-year old natural beauty. Before moving to Philadelphia, her roots were from the hard ghettos of Queens, New York; where she was born and raised. After meeting a handsome young drug dealer, Heaven followed her new lover to his hometown and moved in with him; leaving the City that Never Sleeps for the City of Brotherly Love.

Nine months later, her boyfriend's mangled body was found slumped in a dark alley with four bullet holes through his head. However; after her boyfriend's funeral, Heaven decided not to return back to the Big Apple. Instead, she decided to make Philadelphia her new home.

Heaven was the type of woman who did whatever she needed to survive. Ballers, hustlers, entertainers and famous athletes all paid for her dynamic services, and Heaven made sure she never left a paying customer disappointed. No one complained after going to see Heaven and coming back to Earth. And everyone she let visit all came back for more.

"Yes, Tony, what is it that you want to talk about," she said in her sexiest voice. "My father," Tony said, blowing midsize circles of smoke into the air. Heaven sat down on the edge of the desk and looked directly into Tony, Jr.'s dark brown eyes. After a short pause she said, "I told you everything I can remember. Your dad had sex with every exotic dancer in the club at least ten times. The only dancer he didn't fuck was a dancer named Rose. She turned Mr. Perotta down every single time he asked and he really wanted Rose. It was like he was obsessed with her but the more she rejected him the more he wanted a sweet taste of that Rose."

Tony, Jr. smashed his cigarette in the ashtray and said, "What did Rose look like?" Heaven said, "She was really a beautiful, bad-ass chick. She was the most attractive dancer at the club. I must admit on a scale from one to ten, she's a twelve."

Tony reclined back into his chair and said, "That pretty, huh?" Heaven smile and said, "Yeah, very pretty. I wanted her myself. She looked so good I just wanted a taste but she was strictly dickly, so I never got to see just how sweet that Rose was."

Tony was serious because he needed all the information he could get to figure out who had murdered his father, and he didn't want to leave any stones unturned.

"So who do you think got my father to go to that motel that night," Tony said. "Jr. all I know is that your father had a strong sex drive. He enjoyed having sex or getting his dick sucked every day, but he did that here at the club. He didn't have to go to any motel to get fucked. This office was like a suite at the Hilton Hotel. But like I told you before, if there was anybody in the world that could convince your father to meet him at a hotel, it was Rose. He was crazy about her. Mr. Perotta told everyone how much he thought Rose resembled his late wife, and when Rose quit, your father wasn't the same anymore. So yes, Rose is the only person I believe could have gotten your father to that motel," Heaven said.

Tony continued, "What about my cousins? Do you know anything about that situation," he said, taking out another cigarette and lighting it up. "I told you that the night Bunny was found inside that house in Southwest Philly, she left here about an hour earlier with two black guys. I was inside this office doing what I did for your father. When I looked out the window I watched Bunny get inside of a convertible BMW with both men and they drove off.

After I left your father I went back downstairs to work. Later that same night two masked men broke in here, robbed your father and murdered your cousins and Marty. No one saw the two men. All the dancers were downstairs in the club while everything was going on up here. When the cops got here, they questioned everybody, but nobody saw a thing but your father. He thought he had shot one of the robbers but he wasn't sure. And when he sent out his men to find out what they could about the robbery, nobody knew nothing."

Tony inhaled and blew the smoke out of his nose. He was determined to find and kill all the people responsible for slaying the members of his family. He stood up from his chair and walked around the desk. Looking Heaven straight in the eyes he said, "If you find out anything, I mean anything that can help me, I'll pay you $25,000 cash!"

Heaven's eyes lit up like a fat kid inside of a candy store. Money was her favorite thing and she'd do what she had to just to keep it coming in.

"Find out what you can about Rose. Something keeps telling me that she's the person who's behind the two punks who picked up Bunny. And I believe they were the same two punks that came here and robbed my father and murdered my family. And now after hearing about the attraction my father had for her, I'm also a hundred percent positive that Rose is the woman who led my father to that motel and murdered him and his bodyguard. Find that bitch and your money will be waiting for you," Tony said.

Heaven was delighted as she said, "Don't worry Tony, Jr.; I know a lot of people. If I can't find Rose, then nobody can. Just have my money when I do."

Tony, Jr. watched Heaven walk out of the office. What Heaven didn't know was that after she came back with a solid lead, Tony was going to kill everyone involved; including her. His motto was: *No witness, no case.*

Chapter Three
A ROSE AMONG THORNS II

Early The Next Morning...

Outside the Texas Weiner Restaurant on Lancaster Avenue, Braheem was sitting inside his all white Lincoln Navigator enjoying the sounds of his favorite rap group; I.C.H. (Inner City Hustlers). Moments later, Braheem watched as a red Chevy Tahoe pulled up behind his SUV and parked. Two men exited the Tahoe and walked over and got inside Braheem's car; one of the men was holding a black leather backpack.

Braheem slowly pulled off and blended into the moving traffic. He turned off the CD player and looked over at his friend, Levi. His other friend, Josh, was chillin in the back seat. While Braheem continued to drive he paid very close attention to the rearview mirror, making sure that no one was following him. He had learned the game from his cousin Eric and once he had mastered it, Eric decided to step back from the lucrative drug world and let Braheem make his mark.

Eric was still around but he no longer got his hands dirty. He decided to try his hands at legit businesses and he began investing his money into real estate, stocks, bonds, CDs, and Eric was now the owner of two daycare centers. One was located in West Philly and the other one was in North Philly. Within the next two years he had plans on opening five more *Roses Among Thorns* daycare centers around the city.

After Eric had introduced Braheem to his former drug connect, he walked away from the deadly game with hopes of never returning. Unlike Eric, Braheem wasn't ready to call it quits. He enjoyed the money, power, and the respect that came with being in the game; and now he was ready to pick up where his cousin Eric had left off. Eric would now serve as Braheem's personal advisor, making sure his younger cousin did the right things with his money and avoiding the traps of the Feds, cops, snitches and haters. Braheem took all of his cousin's advice into consideration, but at the end of the day he was his own man and would lead his life and crew on his own terms.

Fifteen Minutes Later...

Braheem pulled his Navigator in the IHOP restaurant on City Line Avenue, and he parked it next to a tinted blue Nissan Maxima. The gorgeous female inside the car rolled down the window and said, "The coast is clear," and then she rolled back up the window and waited.

"How much did you bring with you, Levi," Braheem said. "A hundred thousand. Me and Josh will be finished with everything in a few days," he said, passing Braheem the leather backpack. Braheem looked inside and saw the stacks of money filled to the top.

"Make sure y'all have the other hundred thousand in the next few days. I got to see my connect soon and I'm not trying to take him no short money," Braheem said, zipping the backpack up and laying it between his legs. "My cousin Eric left the game and passed it on to me and I ain't trying to mess things up. I need everybody to play their part. Y'all two are my top street lieutenants and I'm counting on y'all to keep this money coming and everything in order," Braheem said in all seriousness.

"Do y'all hear me," Braheem demanded. "Yeah, we got you, Braheem," Levi said. "Don't worry Braheem, we won't come up short the next time," Josh said. "I hope not because if y'all keep this up I might have to find new lieutenants to take y'all place. Page me when y'all ready," he said.

After they all shook hands, Braheem watched the two men get out of his car and get inside of the waiting Maxima. As the car pulled off and disappeared into the circulation of traffic, he got out of his Navigator, locked the doors and walked into the IHOP restaurant.

A petite, white female waitress escorted Braheem to an empty table in the back of the restaurant. After Braheem ordered his breakfast he sat back and waited for his meal. Directly across from him, two young women were sitting at a table, and Braheem noticed one of the girls staring at him. Both women were very beautiful but the one staring at him was the cutest of the two.

Braheem was not a bad looking guy himself. He was a handsome young man with dark wavy hair and light hazel eyes. He was not surprised that the beautiful woman was staring at him because most women couldn't resist him.

The tall, attractive female boldly stood up and approached his table. For a few seconds they both eyed each other down before having any dialogue. "Hi, my name is Heaven, are you eating alone," she said, seeing the iced-out gold Rolex watch and diamond stud earring inside his left ear. "I'm not if you join me," Braheem said, smilingly. Heaven sat down in the empty chair.
"So what's your name handsome?"
"Braheem," he said, sipping on his glass of cold water.
"You said that your name is Heaven?"
"Yeah, you got it right," she grinned.
"So how can I help you, Heaven? I know you didn't leave your girlfriend all alone over there for a hello."
"No, I saw a handsome young man and decided to take my chances," Heaven said.
"Do you always take chances?"
"Only when I believe it's worth my time," she flirted.
"I like that," Braheem blushed.
"Maybe if we switch numbers you can learn to like a lot of things about me," Heaven said ever so sexy.
"I have to be straight up," Braheem said.
"Please do," Heaven said, looking right into his eyes.
"I have a girlfriend," he said.
Heaven started laughing and shaking her head from side to side. "Don't you worry handsome, I'm a big girl and big girls know how to play by the rules," she laughed.
After they exchanged phone numbers, Heaven stood up from the chair and said, "Braheem, do you mind telling me your age," as she looked into his youthful face. "I'm nineteen," he said. Heaven

smiled. Braheem was a young stallion with a mature demeanor, just the way she liked them.

"How old are you," he asked.

"Old enough to show you the difference between a girlfriend and a woman," Heaven said, before winking her left eye and walking back over to the table with her girlfriend.

Braheem watched as both ladies stood up from their chairs and walked out of the crowded restaurant. He looked out of the large window and watched as they got inside of a silver Lexus LS; Heaven was the driver. When the car pulled off Braheem smiled to himself. Heaven was definitely someone he would be hooking up with, he thought. He looked at the piece of paper with Heaven's phone number on it and smiled. It said, *"(215) 545-5454 Heaven, the most satisfying place on Earth. Call me and find out."*

After Braheem's breakfast had finally come, he ate until he was full, paid his bill and tipped the waiter, and then he left out of the restaurant. Joyce had paged him twice but only two things were currently going through his head; getting the rest of his money to pay off his connect and getting to know his new admirer, Heaven.

Braheem got into his Navigator and eased into the City Line Avenue traffic. Once again he started cautiously looking out of his rearview mirror. Under his shirt was a loaded 9mm and he never left home without it. He grabbed the backpack and sat it on the empty passenger seat. As the sounds of I.C.H. blasted out of his speakers, Braheem headed towards his next destination.

Chapter Four
A ROSE AMONG THORNS II

"So what do you think of Braheem," Heaven asked her friend, as she drove down Market Street. "He's definitely a cutie and from the looks of it he's a young baller too," Coffe said.

Coffe and Heaven were best friends. Just like Heaven, Coffe had also worked at the Platinum Club, and they shared a sharp Center City condominium.

Coffe was average height for a woman, standing about 5' 5, and she was a solid one hundred and thirty-five pounds; with most of her weight being in her ass, thighs and her hips. Her short hairstyle accentuated her attractive caramel features and she was sexy, all the way down to her toes.

Coffe grew up on 23rd and Tasker Avenue in South Philly. However, the lure of fast money, older men, expensive cars and independence led Coffe away from the comforts of her home and straight to the unforgiving but also generous streets of Philadelphia.

"He's only nineteen years old," Heaven said, as she pulled up and parked her car in front of Hair Gallery II hair salon on 52nd Street.
"Girl, what you gonna do with that jailbait," Coffe said, as she grabbed her leather Coach bag and opened the door.
"What do you think I'mma do with a nineteen-year-old young man who's definitely at his sexual peak... Fuck the shit out of his young ass and then send him back home to his little girlfriend with Heaven heavy

on his mind," she said, opening her car door and stepping out.

"Girl, stop it. You got me thinking about being with my baby tonight," Coffe said, as they walked into the crowded hair salon.

"Don't worry; I'll make sure your hot ass gets dropped off over there tonight," Heaven said smilingly. "You better," Coffe exclaimed.

Chapter Five
A ROSE AMONG THORNS II

The Maxima parked behind the red Tahoe and Levi and Josh got out.

"Call me when y'all ready for Braheem," the female said. "Give us a few days Edna and we'll be calling you," Levi said, as he and Josh walked over to the Tahoe and got inside. After Edna pulled off they pulled off right behind her and went in the opposite direction.

Edna "Lady Boss" Smith was Braheem's most loyal and dependable soldier. Edna had the looks of a beautiful video model but had the heart of a cold-blooded killer. Edna looked to be around 5'7, and she weighed a solid 130 pounds. She was a honey brown skinned beauty who always kept her short black hair braided. Her sexual preference she admittedly confessed was for women but she was bisexual.

Just like Braheem, she never went anywhere without a loaded pistol on her possession. Edna was Braheem's eyes and ears to the streets, and known to be a tough female gangstress from the West Park Housing Projects. There was one word she lived and would die by... loyalty.

Levi Taylor was a stocky dark skinned, twenty-one-year old hustler from West Philly. He and Braheem had known each other since their days at the Philadelphia Youth Study Center. Levi stood at 6 feet even, weighing in at 200 pounds; which was mostly muscle. Levi was from the bottom section of West

Philly; where drugs, violence and police corruption was a major part of everyday life. When he wasn't selling kilos of cocaine all throughout West Philly, Levi could always be found inside the James Shuller's Boxing Gym.

Boxing was Levi's first love. Levi's famous right hook was the reason why he was a two-time Golden Gloves State Champion.

Joshua Imia Muhammed was a hard-nose street thug from Southwest Philly. Josh was a twenty-year-old Sunni Muslim. Josh stood 5'10, weighed 175 pounds, with a honeybun brown complexion and a full beard. Southwest Philly was his branded territory. However, Bartram Village, 49th Street, 58th Street, 59th Street, 60th Street, Chester Avenue, Woodland Avenue, and Baltimore Avenue were just a few neighborhoods where Josh's name rung bells as well. Many knew that it was better to be his friend than his enemy, and others had to learn that lesson the hard way.

Braheem and Josh had also met while serving time at the Philadelphia Youth Study Center. They later served time at Glenn-Mills and Slayton Farm boys' homes. While there, they became the closest of friends. Josh was a smooth talking manipulator who loved chasing money and beautiful women. He had been shot three times in the stomach but luckily lived to tell about it.

Violence was nothing new to Josh. He had witnessed his older brother get gunned down right in front of his crying eyes, saw his mother fall victim to her crack demons, and watched his father get sentenced to a thirty-year state bid for armed robbery.

Joshua Imia Muhammed already knew that he would never reach the age of twenty-five. That's why he lived his young life on the edge and was prepared to see Allah whenever his time was up.

Chapter Six
A ROSE AMONG THORNS II

Later That Afternoon...

Rose had just finished her final class of the day. She got inside of her red BMW and drove to the *Northside-Roses Among Thorns* daycare center. After making sure everything was in order she got back into her car and drove to West Philly to check on the *Westside- Roses Among Thorns* daycare center.

Billy watched as Rose pulled up and parked in front of the building. His eyes lit up with joy, and so did hers when Rose saw her little handsome friend staring at her from the window. Rose grabbed her Versace purse and walked inside.

The first person to meet her at the door was Billy. "Hey, cutie," Rose said, smiling and gently pinching Billy's cheek. "Hey, Ms. Rose," Billy blushingly said. "Why it take you so long to come today," Billy said, concerned and anxiously waiting for his answer.

Rose smiled as she walked into her office, as Billy followed closely behind. "I'm sorry handsome, but Ms. Rose had to run a few errands today. You're not mad at me, are you," Rose asked, sitting down at her desk. Billy sat down in the empty chair beside her and said, "No, I'm not mad. I just don't want nothing bad to happen to you."

Rose saw the serious expression on his face and stood up from her chair. She walked over and shut her office door. Rose sat down beside Billy and said, "Billy, tell me what's wrong." Billy looked into Rose's eyes and said softly, "I had a dream that some bad men came to get you, Ms. Rose. But I wouldn't let them take you," he said, feeling better that he had shared his thoughts with her.

"Oh, Billy, don't worry about me. I'll be fine," Rose said as she smiled. She rubbed her soft hands through Billy's curly black hair and tried to comfort his fears. Billy reached into his pants pockets and pulled out a small white piece of paper. He passed it to Rose and she read it.

To Ms. Rose, the prettiest lady in the whole wide world
Love, Billy.

Rose smiled. "Thank you, Billy," she said, reaching over and giving him a huge hug. Billy stood up and walked over to the door. "I'll see you later, Ms. Rose. I gotta go before Mrs. Nelson come looking for me," he said before walking out the door and closing it behind him.

Every day Rose came to the daycare center she looked forward to seeing her handsome young friend. Little Billy Jackson lived a few blocks away from the daycare center with his grandmother because both of his parents were drug addicts. When Billy was born, his mother and father tried to sell their newborn on the black market for three thousand dollars. When that didn't work, they dropped him off at his mother's handicapped mom's house; and neither parent ever came back. The drugs had a hold on them and their addiction was too powerful for either to escape.

When the daycare first opened, Billy's grandmother immediately took advantage of the affordable cost and convenience. Billy was one of the brightest students at the center, and all the teachers there enjoyed his jubilant presence.

The daycare was a large three-story building where a hundred and fifty children, from the ages of two to ten years old, would gather five days out of a week for care. Twenty-five staff members were employed to ensure nothing went wrong. The center was very popular and parents had to wait at least a year to get their children on the waiting list.

Rose was typing on her computer when someone knocked on the door.

"Come in," she said. Eric opened the door and walked inside. His hands were behind his back but she could tell he was hiding something.

"Surprised to see me," Eric said, walking over and giving Rose a dozen long stem red and white roses.

Rose stood up from her chair and hugged him. They embraced with a long loving kiss. She put the flowers inside an empty glass vase sitting on her wall unit and walked back over to Eric.

"What brings you by here today," Rose said as she smiled. "The owner can't come by and check on his business," Eric said. "Anytime, Boss," Rose said jokingly. "I have some good news," Eric said, grabbing Rose's hands. "What is it," she asked. "I just left the appeal lawyer's office and he decided to take on your father's case," Eric said.

"What... Oh my God Eric! Thank you! Thank you! Thank you so much baby," Rose exclaimed, as they started kissing again.

"We're gonna go to the prison this Saturday to see your father. By then the lawyer should have already contacted him," Eric said.
"Baby, I don't know what to say. Thank you so much," Rose said, as a flow of tears ran down her face.

"Just keep praying for your father and God will do the rest," Eric said, holding Rose in his strong and comforting arms. After another long passionate kiss, Rose walked over to the door and locked it.
"This is a cause for a celebration," she said, sliding off her dress and letting it drop down to the floor.
"You can't wait until tonight," Eric teasingly said.
"Call this an appetizer but know when you I get home you will get a hearty main course," Rose said, walking her semi-naked body up to Eric and pulling down his pants.

Rose bent across her desk and Eric took off her panties and penetrated her from behind. Her soft moans began to escape from her mouth. In the comfort of her office, Rose and Eric made passionate love; each lost in a world of endless pleasure.

Chapter Seven
A ROSE AMONG THORNS II

Northeast Philly
Later That Evening...

Braheem parked his Navigator in front of the small two-story row home, got out of his car and went inside. The house was Braheem's private getaway and no one knew about its existence except Eric. The house was located on a small, quiet street. The neighbors on both sides of the house were caucasian and elderly; exactly the way Braheem preferred it. No one would ever suspect that a major drug dealer lived in the house.

Once or twice a week, Braheem would show up at his house and disappear inside. His neighbors all thought that Braheem was a sweet, young college kid; but if only they knew his true profession.

Braheem entered inside his small cozy home and walked upstairs into the bedroom. He tossed the leather backpack on top of his bed and walked over to the closet. Inside the closet was a rack of new jeans and shirts. About twenty-five boxes of brand new Nikes, Adidas, Fila's and Timberlands boots were stacked up against the walls. On a shelf were two loaded 9mm, a tech-9 machine gun, an AK-47 machine gun, a bulletproof vest and several boxes of ammunition.

Braheem grabbed a pair of blue Guess jeans and a white Polo button-up shirt. He tossed the clothes on the bed, along with a new pair of Timberland boots.

After taking a soothing warm shower and getting dressed, Braheem grabbed the backpack full of money and walked downstairs to the basement. A large Maytag washer and dryer sat alongside the wall. Braheem walked over and lifted the top to the washing machine up. The inside of the washing machine was completely gutted out because its purpose was not intended for cleaning clothes. Inside the machine were large stacks of money. The dryer had been redesigned the same way; gutted out and filled up with stacks of hundred dollar bills.

Braheem placed the money from the backpack into the washer and pulled the lid back down. Then he walked upstairs into the decorative living room and sat down on the couch. Braheem grabbed the remote to satisfy his boredom and turned on the Sony flat screen TV.

When he heard his cell phone ringing, he looked on the caller ID to see who it was. It was Joyce, the love of his life. Her jealous, over possessive ways were driving him crazy. Braheem had many female friends that he enjoyed having sex with but his girlfriend Joyce was his one true love. But things were never easygoing with the two. When they weren't making love, they would be arguing and fighting.

Braheem felt the vibration on his pager and checked to see who was calling. A smile came to his face when he realized it was Joyce, who was now using the emergency distress code: 999-111. Braheem laid down his cell phone and pager. As much as he missed his beautiful, sexy woman, he was determined not to call her or show up at the house until he put some space between them. He figured a good five-day separation period would teach her to cut out her jealous ways and give their relationship the peach he desired.

Eric had taught Braheem everything he knew about hustling, money and women. "Patience, control, and determination will help you reach all your goals," Eric told him one day. Braheem had big dreams and he was determined to accomplish every last one of them. He was only nineteen years old but in many ways Braheem was a man that was many years ahead of his time.

Chapter Eight
A ROSE AMONG THORNS II

Joyce slammed down the cordless phone and frustratingly got up from off the bed. "Nigga, why the fuck ain't you calling me back," she said. Joyce grabbed her jacket and walked downstairs. Her son Ryan was asleep on the couch. Joyce woke Ryan up and quickly got him dressed.

"Mommy, where are we going," he said.

"I'm taking you over Grandma's house," Joyce said, putting on his coat. A big smile came to Ryan's face. He loved being over his grandmother's house. His grandmother and two young aunts, Brandy and Aiesha, showered Ryan with endless love and he couldn't get enough of it.

Joyce and Ryan got into her new Audi and drove over to her mother's house. After Joyce dropped off her son, she got back into her car and drove off. Joyce was tired of sitting in the house crying while she waited for Braheem to call or walk through the door. She called Rose on the phone and told her that she was on her way over.

Once she got to Rose's house, the two of them sat on the sofa talking. Eric was inside his home-office going over some important paperwork that he had gotten from his lawyer, so that had plenty of privacy. Rose and Joyce sat back sipping on cold Coronas with lemon, and Joyce tried her best to hold in her frustration. Rose did what she could to comfort her girlfriend, but Joyce was so madly in love with Braheem that every time she mentioned his name, the tears fell from her worried eyes. Joyce was a beautiful woman and she could have any man she desired, but she had given her heart to Braheem. He was the only man who completed her mentally, spiritually and knew how to satisfy her sexually.

Since the night they murdered Mr. Perotta and his bodyguard, Joyce and Braheem had become inseparable. They moved into a large beautiful home in the Overbrook section of West Philly and things quickly heated up between the two. Braheem showered Joyce with all the gifts money could buy. He purchased her a new Audi sports car, the finest designer clothes, jewels, a house and gave her plenty of money. He even treated her four-year old son Ryan like he was his own. Together they all went to Disney World, where Ryan had the best time of his life, and they spent many weekends in Miami or in Atlantic City. Braheem constantly spoiled his family with the finer things in life. He was the man Joyce had always wanted, and the father and mentor that Ryan needed.

"Why won't he call me back, Rose," Joyce said crying. "It's been three whole days since he left out the house," she continued. "Joyce, first you need to calm down. I told you that Braheem is strong. Eric talked to him. You need to be patient and stop stressing yourself out," Rose said. "That boy loves you, girl. And just like you're thinking about him I'm sure he's doing the same thing," Rose said.

"Do you think he has someone else," Joyce said, wiping her tears away and taking another sip on her Corona. "Who knows? Braheem is a very handsome man who has plenty to offer for a woman.

I'm sure a lot of women find him attractive. Look, all I know is that a man will be a man. Joyce it's almost impossible to change their ways but if he loves you he ain't going nowhere," Rose said.

"But you changed Eric. He left the drug game. He gave it all up for you," Joyce said. "No, you're wrong. Eric chose to leave the game alone. It was his decision to walk away. But when Eric was selling drugs, I didn't bother him. I wanted him to know that living that dangerous lifestyle made me feel way uncomfortable but I couldn't force him to leave it alone. Listen, as long as Braheem takes care of home, treats your son like his own child, and pleasures you the way you like, why constantly stress yourself out over things that don't even matter, "Rose said. "I don't want no other chick with my man! I don't know what I would do without Braheem in my life," Joyce said.

Rose stood up from the sofa and walked into the dining room. Moments later she walked back holding her notepad full of poems. She sat back down and flipped through the pages. "Remember this," Rose smilingly said, showing Joyce the poem. "*The Daisy That Grew From Dirt*. Yeah, you wrote it for me. How could I ever forget it," Joyce grinned.

After flipping through a few more pages, Rose found the poem she was searching for. "Here it is," she said. "What's the name of this poem," Joyce asked. "It's called, *The Circle of Eternal Love*," Rose said. "Read it. I want to hear it," Joyce said. Rose sat back on the sofa and began.

The circle of eternal love
Is a circle that can never be broken
It protects love from all outside intruders
It will overcome all obstacles
And persevere through all adversity
The circle of eternal love is timeless,
endless, and unbreakable
It cannot be moved, shattered or blemished
No harm will ever penetrate it.

Joyce sat there as tears streamed down her face. "Rose, that was so beautiful," she said. "Joyce, the meaning of the poem is that no love that's true and genuine can be tarnished. If you and Braheem's love is strong and solid, and y'all are true soul mates; nothing or no one can break through y'all circle of eternal love. That's the type of love my parents have for each other, and the love me and Eric share also. When we get married I will respect him and live by my marital vows, and our circle of eternal love will be even stronger. You and Braheem have a special relationship too, but only time will tell if the circle of eternal love that surrounds y'all, can withstand all the stones and temptations that the devil will throw at y'all."

Joyce leaned over and gave Rose a long hug, as Rose's words penetrated and lingered in the depths of her crying soul. She knew that she could not change her man. She knew she would have to wait and see if she would be the one that Braheem would create a circle of eternal love with.

Chapter Nine
A ROSE AMONG THORNS II

Later That Night
While The Soft Raindrops Fell Down From The
Dark Sky...

Edna was sitting on her couch counting money when she heard a car pull up outside of her apartment. She reached for her loaded 9mm and walked over to the window. As she peeped out of the window to see who it was, Edna's first glimpse was of a silver Lexus LS. Edna smiled and rushed to her front door to open it. It was her new girlfriend, Coffe, whom she had met a few weeks earlier.

Coffe stepped out the car, said a few words to her girlfriend Heaven, then watched as Heaven beeped the horn and slowly drove off down the dim street. Coffe walked inside the house and shut the door behind her. Edna laid her gun down on the table, and then she and Coffe began kissing intensely. Within just a few short weeks, Edna already had her new girlfriend sexually turned out.

In the heat of the moment, the two did not need any words to describe what each other wanted. The two women started removing each other's clothes. Once they were undressed, Edna stood behind Coffe, and softly kissed her neck and shoulders.

"What took you so long," Edna said, grabbing Coffe's hand and leading her to the bedroom. "Me and my girlfriend had a few things to do today. We went shopping, plus I got my hair and nails done...so I could look pretty for you," Coffe said, getting on the bed.

Edna stood at the edge of the bed watching as Coffe spread her legs apart and started playing with her pussy. She watched as Coffe took her fingers out of her juicy, warm pussy and placed them deep inside of her mouth.

"Miss me, baby," Coffe said seductively. "You can't tell," Edna said. "No, show me," Coffe said, sticking her two fingers back into her wet pussy.

Edna rushed over to Coffe and joined her on the bed. She put Coffe's legs on her shoulders and began eating her pussy. Edna ate Coffe's pussy better than any man or woman had ever done before. Coffe's soft and colorful moans filled the bedroom as the flow of orgasms swept throughout her trembling body.

After Edna finished sucking the ever flowing juice from Coffe's pussy, Edna reached under the bed and pulled out an 8 inch strap-on dildo. She strapped up and turned Coffe around onto her stomach. Then without any warning or hesitation, Edna thrust her hard and stiff dildo into Coffe's waiting pussy.

"Mmmm, Ohhh... Ahhhh," Coffe said, as Edna stroked deeper and harder insider of her pussy. Edna had Coffe climbing up the walls, clinging onto the sheets, screaming, grunting, and moaning.

After Edna had sexed Coffe's brains out, she lay back on the bed and let Coffe return the favor.

The two sexed each other like it was their last day on earth. The rain continued to gently dance on the window pane; playing the lover's a sweet, sensual melody.

Chapter Ten
A ROSE AMONG THORNS II

Two Days Later
Wednesday Afternoon
Southwest Philly…

"Fuck Braheem. Who the fuck that nigga think he is,"" Willie shouted. "If he think he's the only one whose gonna eat while the rest of us starve, he's in for a rude awakening!"

Willie stood up at the head of the table and looked at his two young killers. Frustration was plastered on his dark round face. The two men watched as Willie paced back and forth across the room. No one said a word as Willie continued to vent out his anger.

"That nigga has taken two more buyers from me! If this shit keeps happening I won't have nobody to sell my work to. Braheem is stealin all my fuckin customers away. If I can't get rid of my cocaine, then what's the use of having it," Willie shouted. "Fuck Braheem, Edna, Levi and that fake ass Muslim Josh! I'm tired of sitting back watching my money disappear. It's time to go to war! I need them all out of my way now!

Lance, I want you and Sanchez to get those AKs ready. Game time is over fellas. It's time to see if Braheem and his crew is ready for war," Willie said, grabbing his leather jacket and walking out the room.

Lance and Sanchez stood up from the table and followed Willie out of the house. Willie got into his black Nissan Pathfinder and sped off down the dark street. Lance and Sanchez got inside of a grey Ford Taurus and drove off in the opposite direction. Willie Scott was a sturdy, dark skinned man with a volatile methodology. Willie was twenty-six years old and the boss of a small crew of street thugs and drug dealers. Violence was always his way to handle people who stood in his way. He was not a very diplomatic man.

At thirteen, Willie had gotten his first homicide. He killed an innocent man because someone dared him to. By the time Willie had reached twenty-one, he had over five bodies to account for. However, each time he was tried for murder, Willie was always acquitted due to the lack of evidence and witnesses.

While growing up in Southwest Philly, Willie and Josh were once good friends. Now the two men were on opposite teams. And the two former friends were now two men who shared nothing but hatred for one another. Willie's number one enemy was Braheem, Josh's street boss; so you can see how the two would have a problem.

Willie's theory was once you cut off the head, the rest of the body will fall and crumble; and he knew just who could assist him at getting at the head. Lance and Sanchez were Willie's two flunkies. Whatever Willie told them to do, they did.

Lance was a tall light skinned thug who dropped out of the ninth grade to enroll into the violent drug game. Lance specialized in extortion and kidnapping. Sanchez, his partner, was a short, half black-half Puerto Rican menace to society. Out of the three of them, he was the most violent and reckless. Sanchez was only 5' 4, but he possessed the heart of a lion. Fear was not an emotion he possessed, but murder, drugs and sex were his favorite things.

"I need a favor," Sanchez said, lying back in the passenger seat. "What, nigga? Don't tell me you want to see that bitch again... I just took you over there to see her yesterday," Lance said, driving down Chester Avenue. "Come on man, you can pick me up later, right before we go take care of that business for Willie," Sanchez said. "Man, one of these days, Shanika is gonna get you in a lot of trouble," Lance said, turning the Ford Taurus around.

"That bitch is the biggest whore in West Philly," Lance laughed. "I hope you strap up with that bitch. You know she real fertile with all them damn kids she got running around the house," Lance said, as he began laughing loudly. "Yeah, I heard one of them little bastards is yours," Sanchez jokingly said. "Yeah, right. I paid that whore to get rid of mine," Lance said, as they laughed simultaneously.

Twenty minutes later, Lance pulled up in front of Shanika's house. Shanika had her head propped out of the upstairs window.

"I'll be right down," she yelled out, as she headed towards the door. "Yo, just call me when you ready for me to come pick you up," Lance said, shaking Sanchez's hand. "Peace out," Sanchez said, fixing the pistol he had under his t-shirt before getting out of the car.

Sanchez watched Lance drive down the street and when he turned around, Shanika was standing in the doorway with nothing on but her bra and panties.

Chapter Eleven
A ROSE AMONG THORNS II

Inside The Rosemont Cemetery…

Eric stood in front of the large tombstone as tears slowly fell down his face. Inside Eric's hands were a dozen red long stemmed roses. Once a month, Eric would drive out to the cemetery and visit Mike's grave. The cemetery was empty and tranquil. Eric laid the roses across Mike's grave and then he got down on his knees.

"I miss you so much, Mike. I wish you was still here to see what I done with these daycares. I got two right now but me and my lawyer are in the process of buying more property. I'm going to build five more daycares around the city," Eric said, pausing for a moment to wipe his tears away.

"I'm gonna make sure your dreams live through me, Mike. I want you to know that I left the game alone for good. I wish I would have left sooner and then maybe you'd still be here. Me and Rose is getting married next year, right after she gets her degree. Mike… Mike, I miss you, man," Eric cried out.

Eric somberly stood up and shook his head. After a long sigh, he turned and walked towards his car. Slowly he drove away, as the tears of pain and sorrow continued to fall down from his eyes. He wished he could have changed the grave outcome of Mike's reality; but reality was he was gone forever.

Chapter Twelve
A ROSE AMONG THORNS II

Wednesday Night...

The Platinum Club was filled to capacity. Men from all around the city had come to check out all the beautiful exotic women that worked and danced at the popular club. Gorgeous women of all races, colors and sizes moved throughout the club in tight-fitted skimpy outfits.

Tony, Jr. cautiously looked around the club, admiring his money-making establishment. Tony, Jr. and two of his most loyal bodyguards stood on the balcony that overlooked the entire club. Rocko and Knuckles were Tony, Jr.'s two 6' 6, 300-pound bodyguards. He never went anywhere without them. They had both worked for Tony, Jr.'s father before he had been killed mysteriously.

Tony, Jr. watched closely as the men all crowded the stage to watch Heaven perform. She had the crowd of hungry men hypnotized as her gorgeous, naked body flowed across the large stage. As she made love to a long shiny pole, their temperatures rose and so did their dicks. When she had finished her half hour performance, her girlfriend, Coffe, had to come on stage to help her pick up all the loose bills that were scattered around.

Tony, Jr. thought Heaven and the rest of his exotic dancers were all beautiful women, but unlike his father, he didn't sleep with his employees. Tony, Jr. knew that business and pleasure did not mix well.

He personally interviewed every dancer that applied for a position in his club, but sex was never his motive. With them all he saw was money.

Tony, Jr. and his bodyguards were now standing right outside the dancers' dressing room. When Heaven and Coffe walked out, he asked to speak to Heaven alone. Heaven gave Coffe her car keys and told her to wait for her by the car. Coffe quickly walked out a side door that led to the employee's parking lot.

"Yeah, what's up," Heaven said.
"First, I just want to congratulate you on a wonderful performance tonight,' Tony, Jr. said. "Thank you. I try my best to keep the customers coming back," she said, now smiling. "On a more serious note, did you find out anything about that girl Rose yet," he asked. "Not yet, but I still got my ears to the streets. I also spoke with the dancers and if they find out anything I told them I got a stack for the info; so you know they are looking out as well. But I'm sure me or Coffe will find out something soon. Like I said, you'll be the first to know. I gotta run because Coffe is waiting for me to drop her off at her boo's house. See you tomorrow," Heaven said, as she walked away.

Tony, Jr. watched Heaven walk out of the door. When she disappeared, Tony, Jr. and his two bodyguards walked on. Heaven got inside her Lexus and slowly pulled out of the parking lot.

"What was that all about," Coffe said, turning down the music. "He asked me about Rose again," Heaven replied. "Do you think Rose really had something to do with killing Mr. Perotta?

46

When Rose worked at the club she was one of the sweetest girls I knew and she seemed so innocent," Coffe said. "Those are the ones you gotta watch. The Miss. Goody Two-Shoe quiet ones! For real, I don't know if she had anything to do with it or not but for twenty-five thousand dollars, I really don't care either. Sooner or later, somebody will find out something about her," Heaven said, stopping her car at a red light.

"Didn't she meet some baller who paid for her to go back to college," Coffe said. "Yeah, I forgot about that. I asked a few people that live in the projects Rose used to live in about her, but they all said that Rose got engaged and she and her family moved out. Nobody knows where she moved to," Heaven said. "Maybe she moved out of the city," Coffe said. "Twenty-five thousand dollars tells me Rose is still in Philadelphia. I just have to get a location on her. She's my money ticket right now," Heaven said smiling, as she pulled off when the light turned green.

Twenty minutes later, Heaven pulled up in front of Edna's house. Coffe got out of the car and waved goodbye. Then she walked inside where her new lover had been patiently waiting.

Chapter Thirteen
A ROSE AMONG THORNS II

Lewisburg Federal Prison...

Johnny Ray sat on his bunk still shocked about the attorney's letter that he had received in the mail earlier. Eric had paid for a new attorney to represent him on his appeal. It was the best news that he had heard in the last six-and-a-half years of being incarcerated.

The lawyer had already reviewed Johnny Ray's file and he believed that his case had substantial issues that Johnny Ray's first lawyer had overlooked. Now his new lawyer was preparing the case for the Federal appeals court.

As the excitement continued to run throughout Johnny Ray's body, he lie across his bunk and let his emotions give way to a stream of tears. When Johnny Ray was first sentenced to life in prison, he thought his world had come to an end. Every day seemed dark and gloomy. The only light he had shining his way was from his family. They were the one thing he needed to stay alive. With them, Johnny Ray never gave up hope and they encouraged him to never stop believing in the possibility of freedom; and to keep his faith.

God played a significant role in his life and Johnny Ray believed that through God all is possible. Before Johnny Ray closed his tearful eyes for the night, he said a long, silent prayer, to the man above.

Chapter Fourteen
A ROSE AMONG THORNS II

When Braheem walked into the house, Joyce was sitting on the sofa listening to the beautiful voice of Whitney Houston. Ryan was soundly asleep inside of his bedroom. Braheem took off his jacket and laid it across the arm of the sofa. The ceiling lights were all dimmed. A large scented candle sat on top of the glass coffee table.

Braheem sat down on the sofa and grabbed Joyce's hands. He looked into her watery eyes and saw all the pain his absence had caused. Braheem reached out and wiped away her tears. He pulled Joyce into his arms. For a few seconds they both stared into each other's eyes. Joyce grabbed the remote control and turned down the music.

After an elongated pause, she looked into Braheem's eyes and said, "Why do you keep doing this to me? Why Braheem? Why do you keep taking me through this shit? I'm tired of finding females' numbers in your pockets. I'm tired of you running off after every argument. I'm tired of you leaving me in this house all alone. I'm just tired ... tired of being in love with you," Joyce said desperately.

Braheem reached out and wrapped his arms around Joyce. They embraced in total silence, while his arms clutched her warm, soft body.

"Why do love have to hurt so much," Joyce whispered into his ear. "It don't, baby, people make love hurt," Braheem said. "But love can heal also," he said delicately. "Can you please show me...? I'm tired of using your replacement," Joyce said, referring to the vibrator she had hidden under the mattress. "Can my man heal me tonight," she said looking into Braheem's eyes.

Braheem grabbed Joyce's hand and they stood up from the sofa. In one smooth motion, he lifted Joyce up into his arms.

"I hope your replacement didn't drain you because I have a lot of energy tonight," he said, carrying Joyce up the stairs. "Don't you worry, I'll be able to handle it," Joyce said.

When they entered their bedroom, Braheem laid Joyce across the bed. Joyce quickly took off his white t-shirt and tossed it to the floor. Then Braheem watched as she slid off her red thong. Joyce turned around on her stomach and popped her fat, round ass in the air.

"I'm waiting," she said in a soft seductive voice. Braheem stood at the edge of the bed taking off the rest of his clothes. Joyce watched him through the large headboard mirror and she was wet with anticipation. Braheem climbed on the king size bed and joined her. "No foreplay... I'm already ready," Joyce said.

Braheem positioned himself between her legs and slid his hard dick inside her alluring pussy. As his stiff, strong dick made impact with her wet pussy, the moans of pure bliss filled the night air.

Chapter Fifteen
A ROSE AMONG THORNS II

Scooter's Bar
Lancaster Avenue
West Philly...

Scooter's Bar was a common place where all the hustlers and good-looking women would hang out. The place was small but very popular. Levi and Josh were standing outside the bar talking to two attractive females. Their red Tahoe truck was parked in front of the crowded bar, blasting the sounds of rap music from its woofers.

Parked across the street from the bar was a grey Ford Taurus. Inside, Lance and Sanchez watched as Levi and Josh mingled with the two females. They watched as the two women smiled and got inside the truck, before the quad drove down the street.

Lance and Sanchez closely followed behind them. When the Tahoe stopped at a red light, the Ford pulled up closely beside it. Levi and Josh were too busy talking to the women to notice the window of the Taurus slowly coming down. One of the females happened to glance out of the window and noticed the Spanish looking guy positioning an AK-47 machine gun.

"AW SHIT HE GOT A FUCKIN GUN!!!" Her voice was quickly silenced by the raging bullets that were now ripping through the Tahoe's metal.

Levi quickly hit the gas, running through the red light while the men in the Ford gave chase. Shattered pieces of glass filled the inside of the truck as Levi weaved through the traffic, trying his best to avoid the oncoming gunshots.

POP, POP, POP!!! Sanchez kept shooting at his target. Josh had his 9mm pointed out the window returning fire at his assailants. Cars quickly pulled to the side of the road to avoid the impending trauma. One of the females screamed out "NOOOOOOO," as she realized her girlfriend's head was covered in blood.

After a few more shots rang out, all the screaming suddenly stopped. "Murda! Murda! Murda!" Sanchez yelled out of the window. When they heard the sounds of approaching police sirens, Lance and Sanchez stopped their pursuit and headed in another direction.

Josh tossed his gun before Levi pulled the truck in front of the emergency room at the University of Pennsylvania Hospital. Doctors and nurses quickly ran out to assist the injured party. The Tahoe was mangled with bullet holes. The doctors had to swiftly sort out who had been shot, where were the entry and exit wounds, and whose blood was covering who.

When all the commotion had calmed down, Levi had been severely shot in his leg. Miraculously Josh had made it through the ordeal unscathed. Unfortunately, both of the females passengers had been injured and had succumb to their wounds. They had multiple gunshot wounds to the body and one was killed instantly when shot in the head.

The shooting quickly brought a police presence within the hospital. They were searching for answers but neither man spoke a word. Levi and Josh both knew who had tried to kill them, and even though two innocent females were now dead, the no snitching code on the streets overrode that fact. If the police wanted answers they would have to find them with some good ole fashion police work.

Though the policemen were noticeably upset at the lack of cooperation from either individual, they eventually left. Josh sat inside the visitor's waiting room while Levi had his leg operated on. He tried to contact Braheem and Edna but neither one of them answered their cell phones or pagers. Josh mind hadn't fully digested what had just happened. He sat back lost in thought. He had enemies and they just tried to put an end to his life. One thing did begin to become clear as he sat there. That one thing was that his enemies would now have to pay for their attempt with their lives. He would take nothing less.

Chapter Sixteen
A ROSE AMONG THORNS II

Early The Next Morning
Korman Suites Apartments
Southwest Philly...

When Josh called Edna with the disturbing news, Edna quickly called the Yellow Cab Company to come pick up Coffe. She didn't say much to Coffe besides she would call her soon. When the cab arrived they shared a brief kiss and Edna watched her lover pull off.

An hour later, Braheem and Josh arrived in Braheem's Navigator truck at Edna's. Braheem, Edna and Josh frustratingly sat in Edna's living room. Braheem began to pace the floor. He was obviously angry and infuriated that Willie had sent his two goons after his crew.

"I'm telling you man, that crazy nigga, Sanchez, was shooting at us like a fucking madman," Josh said. "Lance was driving the car while Sanchez was shootin and screaming out the window," he continued. "They went too far! If they looking for a war, then we gonna give 'em one! Edna, I want you to get one of our babies ready. Now it's our turn to strike back," Braheem said.

Edna shook her head in agreement. The babies that Braheem were talking about were his Army-issued hand grenades. Braheem had bought them off the black market just in case a situation like this had occurred.

"If Willie wants to play big, then we gonna let him play with the big boys. Levi's leg is fucked up, and two women who don't have shit to do with us are dead because of those stupid ass fools," Braheem said. "Edna, tell me what you think about all of this," Braheem asked.

"I think this is what Willie wants. He's frustrated that you took away his clientele and if we don't retaliate he'll think we're soft. We have to go at them hard and I mean hard! We don't need a long war though...just something quick, efficient and one that will cause major damage," Edna said sternly, as she was ready to go hard for her team.

Braheem agreed. He knew Edna was right and going after Willie and his crew was the only thing to do.

"I want y'all to get all the guys together. Edna, I'll call you in a few hours. I have to go talk to Eric, and then I'm going by the hospital to see how Levi is doing," Braheem said. "Tell Eric I said hi. I seen him and Rose a few weeks ago down Penn's Landing," Edna said. "No problem, Braheem said, before shaking their hands and rushing out of the door.

Braheem got into his Navigator and quickly sped off. While driving down Linbergh Boulevard, he took out his cell phone and called Eric.

"What's up, Braheem," Eric said, answering his cell phone quickly after seeing Braheem's number displayed on his caller ID. "Eric, where you at," he asked. "I'm at your spot waiting for you. I saw the news this morning, so hurry up cause I have a meeting with my lawyer this afternoon, and I have to meet up with Rose," Eric said. "Cool I'm getting on

the expressway right now. I'll be there soon,"
Braheem said, stepping on the gas.

While Braheem headed towards his secluded
getaway up the northeast, his mind was clouded and
filled with racing thoughts. He knew Willie didn't
play fair but neither would he. And now one of them
had to go…and Braheem had no plans of going
anywhere anytime soon.

Chapter Seventeen
A ROSE AMONG THORNS II

"Rose, since you don't have classes today let's go shopping," Joyce said, talking into her phone. "I can pick you up and we can drive out to King of Prussia," she continued. "Alright, as long as I get back to the daycare before it closes. I have a few things to check on, plus you know I can't go a day without seeing my little Billy," Rose said, as a smile came across her face. "Oh, I forgot about your little boyfriend. How is cutie doing," Joyce said.
"Fine, as long as he gets to see his Rose," she laughed.

"So where's Braheem," Rose asked, changing the subject. "He got a call early this morning, then got up, got dressed, and rushed out the door," Joyce said, sounding disappointed. "Did y'all talk last night," Rose asked. "No, not really. We were both too horny to talk. Five days apart really is too long and talking was the last thing on our minds," Joyce said laughingly.

"I'll tell you all about it when I get there. Let me get dressed...I'll see you in about an hour," Joyce said. "See you when you get here," Rose said, as they ended the call.

Chapter Eighteen
A ROSE AMONG THORNS II

Willie and the members of his crew sat inside the living room of one of his stash houses. Lance, Sanchez, and five other men all listened in as Willie talked.

"Them lucky muthafuckers got away," Willie shouted. "Don't worry, Willie, next time Levi and Josh won't be as lucky; or Braheem and Edna once we catch up to them," Lance exclaimed.
"Those two bitches died and that shit is all over the news," Willie said." Don't worry, Boss, the cops don't know shit! But what are we gonna do next," Sanchez said.

"Tomorrow we are gonna hit them again. I want y'all to shoot up all their drug spots. If I can't make no money neither will they," Willie said.
"I'll meet y'all back here tonight at eight o'clock. I want to put everything together before we attack again," he continued. "What time you say to be back here," one of the men asked. "Eight o'clock, J.T., and don't be late the next fuckin time," Willie said.
"I won't. I just wanted to be sure," J.T. said.

Willie left out of the house and along with Lance and Sanchez; they drove off in his Pathfinder. The other men got into their cars and pulled away as well. When J.T. got into his ride he immediately placed a call on his cell phone.

"Hello," a female voice answered. "Edna, it's me, J.T. I need to see you. It's very important," he said. "I think what I have to tell you will be very beneficial to you and your people," he continued. "Alright, meet me at the corner of 54th and Woodland in about an hour," Edna said. "I'll be there," J.T. said, ending the call.

No one knew that J.T. was Edna's informant. For months, J.T. had been spying in on Willie and his crew. In return Edna compensated him with a very nice monetary compensation. The money was good but J.T. knew he had to be careful because if anyone ever found out about his disloyalty, he was a dead man.

Chapter Nineteen
A ROSE AMONG THORNS II

When Braheem walked into his house, Eric was patiently waiting for him on the sofa. Braheem took off his jacket and sat down beside him. They reached out and gave each other a quick hug.

After a long sigh, Eric looked at Braheem and said, "Now tell me what the fuck is going on!" "Willie and his crew tried to kill Levi and Josh last night after they left Scooter's Bar. Instead, of killing them, they shot up the truck and killed the two females. And Levi's leg is messed up pretty bad from what I hear," Braheem said.

"So what are you gonna do about it," Eric said. "Them niggas tried to kill my friends, Eric. What you think I'm about to do. I'm not gonna let Willie get away with this! This animosity we got towards each other has been brewing for a while but now it's boiled over. One of us got to go," Braheem said angrily.

Eric looked at Braheem. He knew that Braheem's mind was made up, and no matter what he said, he couldn't change it.

"Do you remember what I told you about war and money…they don't mix. A war will only make matters worse. Especially a drug war that will get the Fed's attention. You have to outthink your enemy… the same way I did Perotta and his boys, Larry and Bunny. I used their weaknesses against them.

I know you're ready to go back after Willie with force but every war is not fought with weapons.

Most wars are fought and won with strategic manipulation, way before the guns are brought in. It's your choice though. Braheem, this is your decision to make. I left the game and passed it on to you but you're my cousin first; and I don't want to see you dead or serving a life sentence," Eric said, putting his right hand on Braheem's shoulder.

"Eric, you know that I always respect and value your opinion but this time I got to handle my own business. I already told Edna to get things ready. I don't feel right knowing its people out there tryna kill me and my crew. It was you who told me never run to from your problems, because your problems will never go away. Well, Eric, I'm not running away. I'm strappin up and running towards my problems. I hope you're not upset with me, Eric. Remember, cousin, I learned it all from you," Braheem said.

Both men stood up from the sofa and embraced in a long hug. Eric knew that his words had come back to haunt him.

"Just keep me up to date on what's going on. Will you do that." Eric asked. "You got my word, Eric. Oh, Edna told me to tell you hello," Braheem said, grabbing his jacket. "Tell Edna I said what's up and to keep an eye on you," Eric said, as they walked out of the front door.

Chapter Twenty
A ROSE AMONG THORNS II

Edna and Josh sat inside of her car while they drove towards 54th and Woodland Avenue. When Edna stopped at a red light, Josh happened to glance out of the window and he saw his mother walking down the street, looking like a lost zombie. "Pull over real quick," he told Edna.

Edna pulled the car to the side of the road, and Josh promptly jumped out and ran after his mother. Edna didn't say a word. She knew Josh's mother was deeply strung out on drugs and how much it bothered him to see her that way. Edna reclined back into her seat, with her hand on her loaded 9mm, as she patiently waited for Josh to return.

"Mom, what the fuck are you doing," Josh said, running his mother down and grabbing her by her t-shirt. "Joshua, get your damn hands off of me, boy! I don't care who you are on these streets, I'm still your mother," she said, knocking his hand away.

Josh looked into his mother's tired eyes and shook his head in disappointment. His mother, Gayle, was still attractive but the drugs and wear and tear of the street life was surely taking its toll on her. The long, healthy hair she had once had fell out and it looked raggedy, and she had lost a lot of weight since the last time Josh had seen her.

"You got some money," she said holding out her skinny hand. "No. Why, so you can go run buy drugs with it," he said, disgusted with her request.

"Boy, I'm not gonna buy no drugs. I'm gonna buy me something to eat. I'm starving," she said, sounding very sincere. "Mom, when you gonna get off this shit," Josh said, angrily and frustrated. "Whenever you get off of it first! You ain't no better than me, Joshua. In fact, you're a whole lot worse. It's because of people like you, that got people like me all strung out on this shit! You addicted to the money, like I'm addicted to the crack. You keep the streets supplied with this shit so save all that innocent bullshit for somebody who don't know no better.

Oh, and I heard what happened to you and Levi last night. How do you think I feel knowing that my last child almost lost his life...and two girls lost theirs? Remember when you point a finger at somebody, one point up to Allah and three point back down to you.

Now can I have a couple of dollars to get me something to eat or not," Gayle said, crossing her arms.

After a long pause, Josh went into his pocket and took out a thick roll of money. He passed his mother a new big face twenty dollar bill.

"Here, you better not let me find out you bought drugs with this either," Josh said, giving his mother a hug. "Boy, don't you worry about Gayle. I been on this earth for forty-two years. You just try to make it to my age," she said.

Josh watched as his mother walked away. When she had disappeared he walked back to the car where Edna was waiting. When Josh got into the car Edna didn't say a word. She just put the car in drive and pulled off down the street.

63

Fifteen minutes later, Edna and Josh pulled up and parked on the corner of 54th and Woodland Avenue. Moments later, a short, brown skinned man got out of his car and quickly ran over to Edna's car and got in the back seat.

"What took you so long," J.T. said nervously, as he looked out of the slightly tinted windows. "Skip the bullshit. What do you have to tell me," Edna said, ready to hear the facts. "Alright, well Willie is planning to go after y'all hard. He sent Lance and Crazy Sanchez to do what they did and today we had a meeting at one of the stash houses.

Willie is planning to shoot up all y'all drug spots to slow y'all money down. Everybody knows how much he hates Braheem. Willie blame y'all boss for everything, especially for all the money he's been losing out on," J.T. said.

"That's it," Edna said. "No, I got more. Tonight we are all supposed to meet back at the stash house at eight o'clock, so we can go over what Willie want us to do next. Here," J.T. said, passing Edna a piece of paper.

"That's the address where they'll be at tonight. I'll get there a little late so y'all will have time to do what needs to be done," J.T. said. "What do I owe you for this one," Edna said. "I need five thousand. You know it's worth a lot more, Edna," J.T. said, still looking around nervously.

Edna went into her jacket and took out a stack of hundreds. She pulled off twenty hundred dollar bills.

"Here, this is two. You'll get the rest later tonight, after we make sure everything is taken care of," Edna said.

J.T. snatched the money and put it inside his jacket pocket. "Alright, cool. Don't forget they'll all be there at eight o'clock. I'll see you later on tonight," J.T. said, existing the car and running back to his vehicle. He sped off down the street and quickly disappeared.

"I don't know why you fuck with that snake," Josh said, as Edna pulled off and drove down the street. "I'm not worried about J.T., he's money hungry. He's the type of man who will sell his own mother out to the highest bidder. I just make sure I have the money he wants, so he brings me the info I need. That keeps us all on point, especially Braheem. You know the saying; *Keep your friends close and your enemies closer.* J.T. is the snake that's living inside Willie's barn of chickens, and his information will keep our enemy at bay or better yet, destroy him," Edna said.

"But how can you trust him? If he crosses his own crew he'll do the same to us for the right price," Josh said. "Like I said, Josh, don't worry about J.T., I got it all under control," Edna said, dialing a number on her cell phone.

"Hello," Braheem answered. "I got some great news. Our snake has come through," Edna said. "Good, I'm at the hospital with Levi. You know how much I hate hospitals, but I'll meet you and Josh at your house," Braheem said. "How's Levi doing," Edna said.

"He's fine, still a little shook up from last night but he's a soldier. He'll be okay," Braheem said, playfully pushing Levi's shoulder. "I'll see y'all in a few. Talk to you later," Braheem said

Edna placed her cellphone in her cup-holder and continued to drive back to her apartment.

Chapter Twenty-One
A ROSE AMONG THORNS II

Inside The Platinum Club...

Tony, Jr. sat at his desk looking at the three photos he held in his hand, while Rocko and Knuckles stood by the door. Tony, Jr. called them over and passed them the photos.

"That's the girl, Rose. One of the dancers took a few pictures of her when she used to work here. She gave them to me last night," Tony, Jr. said. "Oh, now I remember her," Rocko said, excitingly. "Yeah, me too!" Knuckles said. "Your father did like Rose a lot. She's the one that kept refusing his offer to sleep with him," Rocko said. "At that time, Rose was the number one dancer here. But so much was going on back then I honestly forgot about her...now I remember when she quit your dad was pissed," Knuckles said.

"She's a pretty girl," Rocko said. "Yeah, very pretty and now I can see why my father was so obsessed with her," Tony, Jr. said. "Why's that," Knuckles asked. "Because this girl Rose does kind of favor my mother. She's a little bit darker, but other than that they have a lot of similarities," Tony, Jr. said.

"But now that I remember her, I also remember her being a very sweet person. She wasn't like any of the other females who danced here. She seemed to have a lot of self-respect," Rocko said.

"Fuck the bitch! That was all a part of her game. She tricked my father into believing she was innocent when all along she was setting him up! Think about it… my father wanted her but she kept refusing, then she ups and quits on him. Then not too long after that, the club gets robbed for two million and then my father is murdered inside of a sleazy fuckin motel!!!

I'm no rocket scientist but I'm no fool either. This girl Rose and a few of her friends set my father up, and right now I bet they're all living the good life; thinking that they got away with the perfect murder," Tony, Jr. said angrily.

"I want y'all two to go out and find whatever y'all can about this bitch. I want her dead! I want her family dead! I want everything she loves dead! She's responsible for my pain and now it's my turn to return the favor," Tony, Jr. said, slamming his right fist down on his desk. "Take the pictures with y'all and see what y'all can find out. I'll stay on Heaven and the rest of the dancers to see if anything comes up. But finding this girl is my main priority. So find her and make sure a bullet gets put right between her eyes!"

Rocko and Knuckles nodded their heads in agreement and quickly walked out of the office. Tony, Jr. stood up and paced back and forth across the room. A deep hatred for Rose boiled inside of him. He was a hundred percent sure that she had orchestrated the entire plan to rob and murder his father.

Chapter Twenty-Two
A ROSE AMONG THORNS II

The University of Pennsylvania Hospital...

Braheem hated to be in hospitals but for his close friend, he knew he had to be there. Doctors told Levi that he would probably never walk the same and that he would need crutches, a walker, or a cane to support him whenever he needed to get around. Braheem looked at Levi's leg as it sat in its cast and disappointingly shook his head. They both knew the truth; Levi would probably never box again. The bullet from the AK-47 had ripped through his flesh, crushed his bone, and damaged a major artery in his leg.

"Look at my fucking leg," Levi cried out. "Look what them niggas did to me, man! My boxing career is fuckin through! I'll never be the champ again with one fucking leg," Levi yelled.

Braheem looked into Levi's watery eyes and said, "I promise you they're gonna pay for this shit! I'm sorry that I can't do more to help ease some of your pain, Levi, but I give you my word, homie. Willie, Sanchez, Lance and everybody in their crew will pay for this. And killing those two innocent girls won't go unnoticed either," Braheem said.

Levi knew that no matter what Braheem would keep his word. They had been friends long enough for him to know that Braheem always said what he meant, and meant what he said.

"Is that why Edna called you," Levi asked.

"Yeah, J.T. has given us some good info. Edna didn't say too much on the phone though, but I'm sure it must be good if she called me," Braheem smiled. "Braheem, just make sure you get those bastards! I wish I could be there to see them die or kill 'em all myself...but the doctors said I have to be here for a few weeks of rehabilitation."

"Don't worry, Levi, you just chill. I'll see you in a few days," Braheem said, shaking Levi's hand. "You make sure you watch the news," Braheem said, as he smiled and walked out of Levi's room.

Inside The King of Prussia Mall Parking Lot...

"Ain't that Rose," Heaven said, looking out of her car window. "Yeah, that's her," Coffe said, watching Rose and Joyce who were carrying shopping bags and getting inside of Joyce's Audi. "You wanna go speak to her," Coffe said.
"Hell no! We gonna follow that bitch and see where she's going. I want to get all the info I can so I can get my twenty-five thousand dollars," Heaven said.

"What a coincidence," Coffe said. "I told you Coffe that you can find any bitch at the hair salon, nailery or shopping mall," she said, causing heaven to burst out in laughter.

When Joyce and Rose pulled out of their parking space, Heaven and Coffe quickly followed behind them.

"Are you gonna let Tony, Jr. know about this," Coffe said. "No, not yet. I wanna make sure I have something to tell him first. If I just tell him that I spotted Rose that won't be enough. Let's find out where they're going. Once we have an address, then we have a secure lead," Heaven said, following Joyce's car onto the expressway.

While Heaven stayed on their tail, all she could think about was the twenty-five thousand dollar reward Tony, Jr. had promised.

Chapter Twenty-Three
A ROSE AMONG THORNS II

A Few Hours Later
Center City Philadelphia...

Inside his lawyer's elegant downtown office, Eric and his Jewish attorney, Steven Steinberg, sat at a conference table talking.

"Eric, the properties you wanted to purchase for the other daycare centers might pose a problem," his lawyer said. "What do you mean," Eric asked, sounding confused. "Now the sellers of the properties are asking for more money than they originally wanted. The first two properties were a steal, but these are different owners and they want what their property is worth. I've been negotiating with them all week long," Steven said.

"Steve, I don't care what it is they want, just get me those damn property," Eric fumed. "Eric, why is it so important for you to buy these particular buildings? What's the big deal," Steven said, inquisitively.

Eric looked at Steve and said, "Unlike you, Steve, I grew up with nothing. I grew up a poor kid from the West Park Housing Projects and my role models were all street hustlers. Everything I ever had I earned it. Where I'm from, drugs, AIDS, murder, and poverty are the norms of life. The black and Spanish kids don't have anyone to look up to. Prison or the grave takes away all our fathers and we are pushed out the door to fight and fend for ourselves, and then we end up locked up in prisons or lying in graves next to our fathers. Every last one of my friends is dead or locked up!

My best friend, Mike, wanted these daycare centers up and running before he was killed. He never lived to see them but through me his dreams will come true. I don't care about making money off these properties. I only want to help my people out the best way I can. Helping the youths with modern-day daycares, computers, books, and good teachers is the only way they will have a fair chance in this cruel, white man's world. So like I said, I don't care what the sellers want for their properties, get them," Eric said, standing up and grabbing his briefcase.

Eric buttoned up his navy Prada suit jacket and then shook his lawyer's hand.

"Steve, we've been doing business for a few years now and we have made a lot of money together. I've taken your advice many times before but this time I need you to trust me. Also, before it slips my mind I want to thank you for referring me to that appeals lawyer. He accepted Johnny Ray's case.

I hope we can continue to work together. I'll be looking forward to your phone call after you seal the deal on these properties. Goodbye, Steve," Eric said, turning away and walking out of the office.

After Eric left, Steve called his secretary into his office.

"Yes, Mr. Steinberg," she said. "Kim, I want you to get the property owners together for a meeting next Wednesday. Tell them that Eric and I have agreed to their terms and we are ready to get this deal done."

Chapter Twenty-Four
A ROSE AMONG THORNS II

This is a prepaid call from a Federal inmate.
If you would like to accept this call…

"Hello," Rose's mother said, as she pressed the number five on her keypad and began speaking into the receiver. "Baby-doll, what's going on," Johnny Ray said to his wife. "I'm just praying daily that God brings you back home to me real soon. Rose and Eric told me the good news and we're all coming up there to see you this Saturday," she said.

"Can you believe it," Johnny Ray said enthusiastically. "Yes, I do. I told you, honey, that our God is a powerful God. All you have to do is have faith and believe in him," she said, as the tears started falling down her face. "God knows I need my husband back home with me and our children. I ain't feel your gentle touch in over six years, and each day that passes only gets harder," she said.

"Baby, don't cry, just keep me in your prayers and keep being that rock I need in my corner. I've seen so many prisoners lose their rock and then their minds go with her. I'm truly blessed that God gave me a wife, a friend, and a soul mate that understands the word love and stuck by her vows. I love you, honey," Johnny Ray said, containing his own tears.

"When the boys come home from school tell them I love them and I'll see y'all all on Saturday."

"Baby, I love you too. I'll make sure I tell them what you said. We can talk more about this appeal situation on Saturday," she said.

When they heard the phone line began to beep, they both knew that the call would soon disconnect.

"I love you beautiful, don't you ever forget that," Johnny Ray said. "How can I? You won't let me and that poem you wrote me constantly reminds me. Now I see where Rose gets it from," she said smilingly.

After saying their goodbyes, they both hung up the phone feeling a sense of hope and love. Rose's mother walked over to the dresser and opened the top drawer. She reached under some t-shirts and took out a white folded piece of paper. She closed the drawer and walked away and sat back down on the bed.

The tears continued to fall down her face. She was missing her husband more than anything in the world. And through good or bad, she would never abandon him or betray him. The love she had for her husband was endless. She never removed her wedding ring from off her finger, and she never let the desires of the flesh control her thoughts and body. If she had to die without ever being touched by another man, then she was prepared to. Her love was for one man and one man only; her husband.

As she sat on the edge of her bed, she unfolded the piece of paper and started reading her treasured poem.

.c You More

I love you more today than I did yesterday
and even more than the day before
Yes, I hear you every time you tell me you love me
but still I love you even more
I love your eyes, I love your nose
I love your smile, I love your tears
But I love you more for just loving me
and for showing me that you care
I love your wrongs and all your rights
I love the loving after all our fights
But I love you more for just loving me
and for being my everlasting light
I love your height and your weight
I love your faults and mistakes
But I love you more for just loving me
and for being a Queen who never breaks
I love your flesh and your soul
I love you for giving me your all
But I love you more for just loving me
and for catching me whenever I fall
I love you more today than I did yesterday
and even more than the day before
Yes, I hear you every time you tell me you love me
but still I'll always love you more.

After she finished reading her poem, she tearfully placed it back into her hidden spot in her dresser drawer.

Chapter Twenty-Five
A ROSE AMONG THORNS II

Across The Street From
Westside- Roses Among Thorns Daycare Center...

Heaven and Coffe were inside the car watching from the window. They had followed Rose all the way from the King of Prussia Mall to their current location. When Joyce's Audi pulled up and parked in front of the daycare, Heaven found an empty parking space directly across the street.

They waited inside the car for about a half hour before Heaven decided to pull off and drive away. Heaven still didn't know why Rose had went inside the daycare but she was planning on finding out very soon. She was determined to get all the information she could on Rose. Coffe wrote down the address on a piece of paper and for now she was cool with what she had.

The only reason Heaven didn't continue to follow Rose around was that she had to hurry up and get herself ready for work. She and Coffe had to be at the club early today, so they could break in two new dancers that Tony, Jr. had hired.

"We'll just come back here in a few days," Heaven said, driving her car down Walnut Street. "When we get everything on Rose we need, Tony, Jr. will pay us that money," Heaven said. "Money! Money! Money! The root to all my evil," Heaven said, as they started to laugh.

While Coffe laughed, Heaven had gotten quiet. She had meant every word she said and there was nothing funny when it came to making money. It was a serious business and she played no games when money was involved.

Inside of The Daycare...

"How's my little handsome friend doing today," Rose asked, because Billy's facial expression was sad. Joyce noticed it also but she didn't say a word. "Not too good, Ms. Rose," Billy said in a sad tone. "Billy is something on your mind," she asked caringly. "No, I'm fine, Ms. Rose," he said, walking away with his head down.

Joyce watched as Rose ran after Billy and grabbed his hand.

"Billy, will you please talk to me, please. You're scaring me. Now tell me what's wrong with you," Rose said, kneeling down to face him eye to eye. "Is everything alright, Rose," one of the teachers walked up and asked. "Yes, Mrs. Nelson, everything's fine," Rose said. "Rose, I'll be out in the car," Joyce said, walking out of the door. Mrs. Nelson saw two children writing on the wall and immediately chased after them.

"Now, Billy, can you please tell me what's wrong with you? Is it because I got here a little late again," Rose asked. "No," Billy said, shaking his head. "Are any of the other children picking on you," she asked. "No, they don't talk about my clothes no more since you took me shopping," he grinned.

"Well, what it is? Is everything alright at your grandmother's house," Rose asked. "Yes," Billy smiled. "Then please tell me what's bothering you," Rose begged.

Billy looked into Rose's caring brown eyes and said, "I ... I ... I ... had that bad dream again, Ms. Rose. The dream where those bad guys try to hurt you. But... But...," he stopped. "But what," Rose said. "But I won't let them," Billy said.

Rose looked into Billy's cute little face and smiled. A tear fell down from the corner of her left eye. "Billy, I told you that I'll be alright. Please stop worrying yourself. Will you do that for me, please," Rose said, reaching out and giving Billy a warm motherly hug. "Yes, Ms. Rose," Billy said, while his head lay on her shoulder.

"You have to promise me, Billy," she said, feeling Billy's tight embrace around her back. "Yes, Ms. Rose," Billy muttered softly. "Yes, I promise."

After Billy went back inside his classroom with the other children, Rose walked outside and got into the car with Joyce.

"What did your little cutie have to say...that he was leaving you for one of those pretty girls in his class," Joyce said jokingly. Rose sat there lost in thought. She hadn't heard a word Joyce said.

"Rose ... Rose ... WAKE UP," Joyce said, jolting Rose back from her momentary daze. "Huh, what did you say, Joyce," Rose said, as Joyce slowly pulled off down the street. "I said what did Billy have to tell you," Joyce asked.

"He said that he had a bad dream and some bad guys were trying to get me but he didn't let them," Rose said, with a perplexed look upon her face. "Joyce, that's the second time he has said that to me," Rose said, fighting the fear that his dreams had now began to grow inside of her.

Chapter Twenty-Six
A ROSE AMONG THORNS II

Southwest Philly...

The black Cadillac stopped at the corner of 55th and Greenway Avenue. Rocko and Knuckles watched as two attractive black women walked across the street. Each held a photo of Rose inside their hands. They stared hard but after the two women had crossed the street, they disappointingly continued on. They had driven all throughout Southwest Philly searching for Rose. But after looking for what felt like ten long and boring hours, Rocko and Knuckles decided to call it a day and go back to the club.

"Finding this broad is like searching for a needle in a haystack," Knuckles said, reclining back into his seat. "Yeah, but Tony, Jr. don't care how long it takes us to find this woman, he wants her dead," Rocko said. "D ... E ... A ... D... DEAD!!!" he continued.

Chapter Twenty-Seven
A ROSE AMONG THORNS II

Heaven and Coffe went by their downtown condominium to pick up a few dance outfits and some shoes. After they got the clothes they wanted, they got back inside Heaven's Lexus and headed straight to work.

"After work I want you to drop me off at Edna's," Coffe said, closing up her cell phone. "Damn ho, that chick got you turned out," Heaven said jokingly. "Don't be jealous that I'm getting my freak on and you're not," Coffe said.
"That's only because I ain't find nobody thorough enough to give it to. I'm gonna call Braheem tonight and see if he's worthy of Heaven's paradise," Heaven smiled. "You ain't call that fine ass nigga yet," Coffe said.

"No, he ain't call me! But I'ma give in tonight and make the first move, cuz I ain't stop thinking about Braheem since they day we met at IHOP," Heaven said, pulling her car into Club Platinum's parking lot.

Heaven parked her car in its regular spot and turned it off. She took out a rolled up blunt and lit it up. Her and Coffe passed the blunt back and forth, enjoying the euphoric feeling that the marijuana gave them.

"So what's up with Edna? What is she into besides fucking your pretty brains out," Heaven laughed, passing the blunt back to Coffee.

"She don't talk much about what she do but I'm almost positive that she hustles. The girl is always counting money," Coffe said, passing the blunt back. "No wonder you stay over there so much," Heaven said. "No, the money has nothing to do with it. I really have feelings for Edna and I'm sure she feels the same for me," Coffe said seriously.

"Well maybe this nineteen-year-old can make me forget all about money," Heaven said. "What," Coffe said, choking on the blunt. "Yea, after I fuck the shit out of him I'll forget all about my money and we can start spending all his," Heaven said, as they started laughing.

7:52 p.m.
The Corner of 49th and Baltimore
Southwest Philly...

The three hooded individuals all sat on their Kawasaki 1100 motorcycles. From a half block away they had all watched Willie and members of his crew walk inside of a house. Though it was night, the full moon lit the sky as well as the many shining stars. The September air was calm and the few people that were outside didn't pay them any mind; they were all too busy getting to where they needed to be. A few cars drove up and down the quiet street but still no one had paid the three hooded bikers any attention. They all waited patiently. Each knowing that tonight was all about murder and revenge.

Inside the stash house Willie stood in the living room waiting for one more of his men to arrive. As he waited, a short dark-skinned man walked through the door. He quickly took off his jacket and sat down with the other seven men that were standing and sitting around.

"Where's J.T. ass at," Willie said angrily. "He's late again," one of the men said. "Willie, do you got a minute. I need to talk to you back in the kitchen," Sanchez said. "Lance, what time is it," Willie said, before walking away towards the kitchen. "It's 7:58," Lance said, looking down at his Movado watch.

Willie shook his head angrily then followed Sanchez back into the kitchen. At that exact moment the three people on the motorcycles drove up in front of the house. Two of them pulled out loaded 9 mm's, while the other went inside their black leather jacket and took out an Army-issued hand grenade.

They all climbed off their bikes and approached the front of the house. Inside the house were boisterous sounds of men laughing and talking. The person holding the live hand grenade pulled the pin out and quickly tossed the grenade through the cracked front window of the house; and it didn't take long for the desired effect to take place.

BOOOOMM!!! The small house instantly shook and flames blazed through the home. The sounds of dying men echoed inside the burning house. A few burning bodies ran out the front door, and each were met by the two hooded gunmen. They plucked them off like flying ducks. Pap! Pap! Pap! Pap! Pap! Pap! They filled their burning bodies with hot lead.

As the screams of death continued to echo in the air, the three bikers quickly got back on their Kawasaki's and sped off into the cover of night.

Inside the burning building, bodies and parts were scattered all around the living room. When the police and firemen arrived on the scene it was horrific, chaotic and no suspects were in range. A large crowd of shocked onlookers couldn't believe their eyes, as the smell of death burned towards the now dark and cloudy sky.

J.T. had been inside his parked car watching as the chain of events took place. As the house burned and the men were shot dead, he sat in his car with a smile plastered on his face. J.T. wanted Willie dead more than anyone. With Willie gone he could take over all of Willie's drug houses and corners. That's the reason why J.T. decided to cross his former friend and drug boss. It was all about money and power.

J.T. watched as the police blocked off the scene and the firemen tried to put out the blaze. Knowing that there would be no one to stand in his way, J.T. thought about his new golden opportunity.

As he started up his car, J.T. pulled out of the parking space and slowly drove off in the opposite direction. He was sure that there would be no survivors left. Now J.T was off to pick up the rest of his money from Edna and plot his next move.

Chapter Twenty-Eight
A ROSE AMONG THORNS II

After Eric and Rose had both enjoyed their delicious seafood dinner at the Red Lobster, they got inside of his Mercedes and headed downtown to the Marriott Hotel. Inside of suite 421 they sat inside of the bubbling Jacuzzi relaxing. Their naked bodies hugged up next to each other as the suite brought back memories.

Suite 421 was the first place they had ever made love and it was Rose's first time ever. Each month they would come back to Suite 421 to rekindle the passion of their unconditional love. It was a day in the month that they each looked forward to.

Rose climbed on top of Eric's body and slid down onto his hard dick as it penetrated deep inside of her thriving love tunnel. She placed both arms around his neck and started riding her handsome fiancé like an X-rated porn star. Her moans escaped from her mouth as Eric's dick grew stronger and thrust deeper inside of her.

Eric cupped his hands around her ass, grunting and moaning every time Rose hips slowly twirled around, and she made her pussy clutch his dick. He gripped one of her breasts and placed it into his mouth. His soft lips played with her sensitive nipple, causing her to peak.

Rose started riding Eric harder and the water from the Jacuzzi splashed to the floor. Rose had become everything that Eric wanted her to be. She satisfied him like no other woman had, and with her he was always turned on.

"Daddy...Daddy, how does it feel," Rose asked seductively, as she continued to ride him. "It... feels ... so damn good!!! Rose," Eric shouted.

Rose leaned down and they started kissing. Steam filled the air and their bodies were wet and hot. She could feel her body on the verge of a wonderful overpowering orgasm. She rode him harder, feeling the length of Eric's dick deep inside of her pussy. Rose started kissing and sucking on Eric's neck.

"Ohhh, Yes! Yes! Yes! Daddy! I'm cumming!!!" Rose screamed out in pure delight. As she and Eric climaxed in unison, the feelings of ecstasy, satisfaction, and love, mixed through their souls as chills swept through their bodies.

Rose slumped down onto Eric's chest. He lifted up her delicate face and softly kissed on her lips before saying, "That's one of the many reasons why I love my Rose."

Chapter Twenty-Nine
A ROSE AMONG THORNS II

Behind the Elmwood Skating Rink
Southwest Philly...

Braheem, Edna and Josh waited by their motorcycles. The back street was dark and quiet. Braheem had a marker in his hand and a serious expression on his face. Hearing his cell phone ring, he took it out of his pocket and answered quickly.

"Yeah, Joyce, what's up," he said. "Where you at? Why you ain't answer the first time I called? What time you coming home tonight? I hope you ain't out there with no other bitch and leaving me in this house by my damn self again," Joyce shouted into the phone.

"Joyce, will you stop tripping, girl! I'm handling some important business right now. I'll see you in a minute," Braheem said angrily.

"You always handling some important business, Braheem! Your ass needs to be here taking care of home," Joyce vented. "Braheem, it's time," Edna said, seeing J.T.'s car coming down the street.

"Who the fuck is that? I know you ain't out with some other bitch, Braheem," Joyce yelled. "Look, I'll be home in a minute. I got to go," Braheem said, closing up his cell phone without any further explanation.

They watched J.T. park his car and get out. He wore a big smile on his face as he crossed the street, but he quickly noticed the stern expressions on all their faces.

"Is everything ok? I told you Edna that they would all be inside the house. I just left. The house is burnt up. Ain't nobody survive that," J.T. said. "Yeah, thanks, but unfortunately I hate snitches, rats, informants, and cowards who ain't loyal to their crew," Edna said, taking her hand from behind her back and pointing her 9mm at J.T.'s head.

"PLEASE DON'T KILL ME," he shouted, hoping that someone would hear him. "I did it for y'all," he cried. "No, you slimy ass nigga, you did it for yourself! You think we don't know you want to take over Willie's empire," Braheem said, pulling out his gun as well. "You ain't getting the chance to sell us out to the highest bidder," Josh said, pulling out his gun too.

J.T. stood there in fear. He knew that his life was over. Before he could beg or say another word, Edna shot him between the eyes and then Braheem and Josh shot him once in the chest. J.T.'s body slumped hard to the ground. Both of his eyes were still open but he was dead.

Braheem turned J.T.'s body over onto his stomach. He lifted up his jacket and shirt and started writing, "NEVER TRUST YOUR FRIENDS!!!" on J.T.'s corpse. It was his way of letting people know that J.T. was a cold-blooded, double-crossing snake. They quickly jumped back on their bikes and sped off.

In the morning the police would discover another dead body and J.T.'s name would be added to the long list of unsolved homicides in Philadelphia.

Chapter Thirty
A ROSE AMONG THORNS II

A Few Hours Later
The University of Pennsylvania Hospital...

Levi laid in his hospital bed in total shock. He knew some shit was going to go down, but he couldn't believe how the news reporter had just described the gruesome scene and the discovery of six dead bodies. A smile came to his face as he rubbed his injured leg. Braheem had kept his word and tore up Willie's crew.

He grabbed the TV remote control and turned off the mounted TV. After a nurse came in and turned off the lights, Levi laid still as he snuggled up under the covers. With his hands behind his head, he stared hard up at the ceiling. "Finally, Willie, Sanchez, Lance and the rest of their crew are dead and out of the way," he said softly.

A part of him still couldn't believe that they were all dead. They deserved what they had got and he knew no one could have possibly escaped the blaze... Or could they?

Levi closed his eyes with the biggest smile dancing on his face. His man had always been a man of his word and Braheem had truly put him at ease. Moments later, the snores of a peaceful man escaped into the air.

Chapter Thirty-One
A ROSE AMONG THORNS II

When Braheem walked into the house, Joyce was sitting on the sofa waiting for him. Brhaeem could sense the tension in the air, and once he saw the angry look on her face he knew it was going to go downhill from there. The day had been a long, stressful one, but he knew that an argument with Joyce was inevitable. Joyce stood up and approached him.

"Nigga, who the fuck was that bitch you was out with," she shouted. Braheem just shook his head without answering. He was tired and sleepy. The last thing he needed was a late night argument or fight with Joyce.

"You heard me! Who was that bitch you was out creeping with," Joyce said, grabbing his arm.

Braheem pulled his arm away and said, "I was out handling some important business. I don't have to explain everything I do to you! Either you trust me or you don't but I'm not gonna go through this bullshit every time I'm working," Braheem yelled back.

"How can I trust you when I keep finding random bitches numbers in your pockets? How can I trust you if I call you and some bitch is calling your name in the background? How can I trust you when you see my name on your caller ID and don't answer my calls? Do you think just because you pay all the bills and fuck me good that I'm supposed to just take your shit and keep my mouth closed," Joyce shouted.

"Do you, Braheem," she continued.

Braheem grabbed Joyce by the shirt and threw her down hard on the sofa. A look of fear instantly replaced her eyes or rage. It was the first time that Braheem had ever used any real force with her. He had her pinned down to the sofa.

"I'm tired of this bullshit, Joyce! I'm tired of coming home every night and going through this! I'm a hustler and you knew this before we got involved! I'm not your son, I'm your damn man! I make sure you and Ryan don't want or need anything! You're a spoiled fuckin' brat, Joyce! That's why so many beautiful women end up with nothing or with niggas that ain't worth shit!"

Joyce sat there as Braheem continued to vent out his frustration. "

"You're beautiful Joyce, but your attitude is ugly as shit! If I didn't love you and your son I would have left you a long time ago. And you're slowly chasing me away and sometimes I don't think you even care because as long as it's about Joyce, nothing else matters. I left for five days the last time and now I'm gonna walk out this door again for I don't know how long. You need time alone, Joyce. Time to get yourself straight," Braheem said, looking into Joyce's watery eyes.

Ryan was awakened from all the commotion and he walked down the stairs. He saw Braheem getting up from off his crying mother.

"Mommy," Ryan said, running into Joyce's arms. Braheem didn't say a word as he walked over to the door.

"Believe it or not, the woman's voice you heard was Edna," Braheem said, opening the front door and walking through it. Joyce sat Ryan down on the sofa and ran after Braheem. She stood in the doorway watching as Braheem got inside of his Navigator. The tears continued to fall down from her eyes.

"I hate you! I hate you, Braheem," Joyce shouted but Braheem didn't respond. He just shook his head disappointingly and pulled off down the street.

Joyce walked back into the house and sat down next to her son. She knew she shouldn't have said what she said, but once again Joyce had let her emotions get the best of her. As Ryan lay cuddled in her arms all she could do was cry and wait for her man to come back home.

As Braheem drove towards his house up the northeast, his cell phone rang. When he looked at the caller ID, he didn't notice the unfamiliar number.

"Hello, who's this," he answered. "Is that how you answer your phone when a friend calls," a sexy voice said. "Stop playing. Who is it," Braheem demanded. "It's me, the woman Heaven you met the other day at IHOP," she said. "Are you busy? Did I call you at a bad time," she continued.

"No, I'm sorry. What's up, Heaven? It's pretty late, ain't it?" Braheem asked. "Not for me. I get off my job late," Heaven said. "Where do you work at," Braheem asked. "How about I give you my address and we talk about whatever you want to talk about when you get here. I'm a little lonely tonight and I could use some company," she said flirtatiously. "But if you have a girlfriend-curfew and can't come, I understand," she laughed.

"A what," Braheem said confused.

"A girlfriend-curfew that comes with having a girlfriend," Heaven said. "No, what's your address? I'm on my way," Braheem said.

After Braheem wrote down Heaven's address, he quickly turned his truck around and headed towards downtown Philadelphia. The traffic was light and twenty minutes later he pulled his Navigator in front of Heaven's condominium.

Heaven was standing in the doorway when Braheem pulled up and parked. Braheem got out of his truck and approached her. Heaven had on a pink see-through nightgown with nothing under it but her Victoria's Secret panties. Braheem could see Heaven's perfect round breasts underneath the gown.

"Hey, cutie," Heaven said grabbing his hand and inviting him inside.

After she shut the door they walked over and sat down on the leather sofa. Braheem looked around the elegant condo and approvingly nodded his head. The place was well decorated and tasteful. Heaven had lit up two large scented candles right before he got there and the aroma was pleasing to him.

Braheem tried his best to keep his eyes away from Heaven's teasing breasts. He looked into her face and she was even more beautiful than the first time they had met.

"So you like," Heaven asked him as she smiled. "Yeah, you have a very nice place here. Do you live by yourself," Braheem said. "No, I live here with my best friend, Coffe, the girl you saw me in the restaurant with, "Heaven said, moving a little closer. "She's not here tonight though. I dropped her off over a friend's earlier. So it's just me and you handsome," Heaven flirted.

"Are you hungry? Do you want something to drink? I have Heineken's, Coronas and some wine in the fridge," Heaven said, showing she was very considerate of her guest.

"No, I'm fine," Braheem said. "So where do you work at," he pried. "I'm a dancer at the Platinum Club," she said. "The Platinum Club," Braheem said shocked. "Yeah, have you been there before," Heaven said, noticing his expression had changed since she brought up the location of her job.

"No, I just heard about it," he lied. "Well, I'm the number one dancer there. Why don't you come out one day and come see me perform. I promise, you won't be disappointed," Heaven said. "Maybe one day. I'm not really into strip clubs," he said.

Hearing the Platinum Club had brought back a lot of old memories. Memories that Braheem tried to erase from his mind.

"What's wrong, cutie? You seem like you have a lot on your mind," Heaven said, grabbing Braheem's hands and moving in closer. "Talk to me. I'm a big girl… I'll understand," she said, staring into his eyes.

"Hold up. Don't tell me. From the look on your face it's a girl problem, ain't it," Heaven smilingly said. "How did you know," Braheem laughed. "It's written all over your face," Heaven replied. "Oh, yeah, then what else can you see," he joked.

Heaven looked into Braheem's eyes. She squeezed his hands in hers and said, "Your girl is probably the jealous type. I'm sure she's a very pretty girl because a man as handsome as you wouldn't have it any other way." Braheem laughed.

"Y'all probably argue all the time about petty shit and..." He interrupted her, "That's enough. What are you a psychic or something," Braheem said. "No, I just know that a girl can't handle a man like you in her life. Either she will run away from you or chase you away from her. See, handsome, girls can't handle the truth, women can," Heaven said looking into Braheem's eyes with a lustful grin upon her face.

"I'm sure you do you out on them streets, but I can also tell that you're the kind of man that takes care of your home and his priorities. A girl can't handle that. They only care about themselves but a woman will let you do you. We know we can't lock down a hustler. When he's ready to be on lockdown, he'll do it himself," Heaven said.

Braheem couldn't deny that this girl had read him to the tee. Right then he knew that this beautiful woman could be a lot of trouble. She was attractive and she knew exactly what he was looking for.

"I'm single and I would really like to get to know you, Braheem. I understand you have someone in your life but that's not my problem, it's yours. I'm a woman who goes after what she wants. When I saw you at the restaurant I knew I wanted you. That's why I approached you. You're nineteen and I'm twenty-six, and even though age don't mean nothing, I'm sure that I can show you a few things that a girl just can't," Heaven said, leaning in closer.

They started kissing. Braheem could feel her soft, round breasts rub up against his chest, and Heaven could feel his hard dick growing inside of his pants. They kissed intensely for five minutes without a break. Both were completely turned on by the other.

Heaven took Braheem's jacket off and pulled his shirt over his head. Then she took off her nightgown and threw it to the floor. Once again their lips locked in another long passionate kiss. While they kissed, Heaven slid down his pants and underwear. Then she slid down her panties. Their lips never separated. When they stood up from the sofa, they were totally naked; and still embraced in a heated tongue dance.

Braheem finally pulled his lips away from Heaven's heavenly lips and started kissing on her neck. As the soothing feeling swept through her body, she returned the favor. They were both excited and filled with anticipation.

Heaven dropped to her knees and gently grabbed Braheem's hard dick. She let her juicy and warm mouth play with the tip of his head. She swallowed him as far as she could go, and then she stopped and stood back up.

"I have condoms in my bedroom. Follow me," she said, grabbing his left hand and leading him back into her cozy bedroom.

Once they entered the lush bedroom, Heaven pushed Braheem down on top of her king-sized canopy bed. She walked over to the light switch and dimmed the lights. Then she opened her dresser drawer and took out a box of Magnum Condoms.

"Here start with one of these but just know that I plan on going through the whole box," she said, smilingly as she tossed him the box. Heaven climbed on the bed and joined him.

"I told you that there are a lot of things that a girl just can't show you. Tonight I'mma show you the difference between how a girl has sex and a real woman fucks," Heaven said, as they started kissing again.

For the rest of the night, until the early morning, Heaven and Braheem sexed each other down with only a few breaks in between. Even though the sex was unbelievable, Braheem's mind did wonder. He thought of Joyce because she was the only woman he truly loved.

Friday Morning...

Heaven sat on the edge of the bed watching as Braheem put his clothes on. Her wonderful night with him had been a lot more than she had expected. Braheem was a nineteen-year-old stallion in bed and he satisfied Heaven in every way her body desired. Now she understood why his girlfriend was so jealous.

Braheem was handsome, young, paid and could fuck like a professional. Heaven sat there with no clothes on, still caught up in the memory of their heat-filed night. Right then she knew she had to have him and she wouldn't let nothing or no one stand in her way.

"You have to leave so soon," she said, walking up to Braheem and putting her arms around him. "Yeah, I got an emergency call so I gotta go handle it. I have to see what's going on," Braheem said.

"Besides, I thought you said that you had to drive by a daycare center to get some information," he asked. "I do but I have to wait for my girlfriend to come back home so we can go together," Heaven said, kissing his neck.

"I'll be back later tonight," Braheem said. "You serious," Heaven said. "As a heart attack," Braheem joked. "Well can I at least give you a going away present until I see you later," Heaven said dropping down on her knees. "I only got a few minutes and…"

Before Braheem had finished his sentence Heaven's moist mouth was wrapped around his dick. Braheem grabbed the top of her head and held on while Heaven swallowed his manhood. When his dick touched the back of her throat, he started to buss. Heaven massaged his balls while her mouth slithered up and down his dick.

In less than three minutes Braheem exploded his thick white cum all inside of Heaven's mouth, and she made sure Braheem watched her as she swallowed every drop. After she licked her lips she smiled and said "All I needed was a few minutes. When you come back tonight I'll make it last longer."

She stood up and looked into his eyes. She grabbed the washcloth from off the dresser and cleaned Braheem off.

"I'll call you as soon as I get off of work. I'mma drop my girlfriend off at her lover's house and then I'll meet you back here," Heaven said, grabbing a towel and washcloth as she walked towards the bathroom. "Just lock the door on your way out," she said.

Braheem grabbed his jacket and walked over to the door. He stopped and turned around. He looked at the messed up bed and all the condom wrappers scattered all over the floor. He smiled to himself as he walked out of the bedroom.

When he opened the front door, Coffe was just getting out of a Yellow Cab. As he walked out the door, they each smiled but kept going about their way. Braheem quickly got into his Navigator and sped off down the street.

Coffe walked into the apartment and looked around. Then she walked into Heaven's bedroom and saw the silk sheets all over the bed and the Magnum condom wrappers all over the floor. She heard Heaven singing in the shower and then she rushed into the bathroom.

"Tell me everything and you better not leave out nothing!!!"

Chapter Thirty-Two
A ROSE AMONG THORNS II

When Josh received Edna's emergency call, he quickly got into his car and headed for her apartment. While driving down Chester Avenue he saw his mother walking with two men. He pulled over and called his mother over to his car.

"Mom, what you doing out here this time of morning," he said, already knowing the answer to his question. "Boy, what did I tell you about asking me dumb ass questions," his mother said.

The two male crack heads stood back not saying a word.

"Who the fuck is these dudes mom," Josh said angrily. "They my good friends, Slim and Pete," she said proudly. "Get the fuck out of here y'all fuckin crack heads," Josh shouted angrily. "We'll see you later, Gayle," Slim said, walking away with Pete close behind him.

"Boy, why you scare my friends off," Gayle said. "Mom, why you out here trickin and smoking that shit? Why don't you let me put you in a rehab again," Josh said sincerely. "Boy, ain't no rehab gonna fix my problems! How can some fat white lady tell me about changing my life around? That bitch don't know nothing about living in pain and poverty! Them drug counselors is getting checks for nothing. I told you to give me the money and don't waste it on that place," Gayle laughed.

"Mom, you have to want to get off of drugs. Look at you... Don't you want to get your life back in order," Josh said in a saddened tone. "Yeah, after you fix yours. I told you about always trying to school me, Joshua. You need just as much fixin as I do. Your mother on drugs and my son a big time drug dealer. We both headed straight to hell," Gayle said seriously.

"All I'm doing is enjoying myself. I ain't hurting or killing nobody but myself. Can you say the same," Gayle asked. Josh didn't answer.

"Yeah, I thought so. I heard about that house getting blown up last night. And I know that house. People in that house was them boys who don't like you. I ain't say nothing to nobody but I keep telling you, Joshua, that ya mamma ain't make it all this far by being no dumb ass crack head. I can put two and two together, Joshua. You just make sure you watch yourself cause sometimes it's the ones you never expect that come back and bite you in the ass," Gayle said.

"Now, since you just ran my friends off who were buying me breakfast, can your dear mother have some money," she said, holding out her hand.

Josh shook his head and went inside his pocket to give his mom twenty dollars. Gayle quickly snatched the money from out of his hands.

"Thanks, baby, I love you," Gayle said, leaning inside the car and kissing Josh on his cheek. "You still my baby boy. You be safe out here on these streets," Gayle said rushing away.

As the sadness swept through his body, Josh drove away. When he looked in his rearview, he saw his mother again standing with Slim and Pete.

Chapter Thirty-Three
A ROSE AMONG THORNS II

Joyce had lain in bed crying all night long. She knew it would be some time before she heard or saw Braheem. She looked at her son Ryan who was sleeping at the foot of the bed. She remembered something that Rose had told her about releasing your trapped emotions through writing.

Joyce picked up her notepad and pencil from off the nightstand. She sat there momentarily consumed with her thoughts. So much had been on her mind. After a long pause, Joyce let the thoughts inside of her crying soul finally escape through the pencil, onto the pad she held inside her hand.

"I Thought You Loved Me ... I thought you really loved me / at least that's what you said. Were those words you spoke all genuine / or were you just playing with my head? If you love me, then why do you run away when times get a little rough? I know that when love is truly real/there is no such thing as, I had enough. Why do you keep playing with my mind and keep breaking my wounded heart? Why do you keep turning out our shining light / and keep leaving me in this dark? You told me that your love is unconditional and together we can fight through it all. You said our love will continue to rise / that real love can never fall. I thought you really loved me / at least that's what you always said. Tell me, were those words you spoke the truth / or were you just playing with my head?

After Joyce wrote down her poem she laid down her pencil and pad. Then she cuddled up next to her son, as the stream of tears escaped from her eyes.

Inside Edna's Apartment...

Braheem and Josh were disappointed about the news they had heard.

"Edna, you sure," Braheem said. "I'm positive. The news said that only six men died. The two out in front of the house and the four burned bodies found inside the living room," Edna said. "They didn't say which bodies were found," Josh said.

"No, they didn't give out any of the names. All they said was there were six dead," she said.

"Damn! Two of them are still alive," Braheem said angrily. "Eight people went inside that house last night. How can there only be six bodies," Braheem said. "Maybe two escaped somehow. It's possible that a few could have been in other rooms when I threw that grenade through the window," Edna said.

After a long pause, Braheem looked at Edna and Josh and said, "We have to find out who survived. We can't have none of our enemies still alive! Everybody needs to stay focused and watch their backs. Soon, whoever made it out of that house will show up; and the next time they won't be so damn lucky," Braheem said.

"Don't worry, I'll find out who survived. I still got a few eyes and ears out on the streets," Edna laughed. "Y'all just be safe. The cops are all over the streets. Don't call me at home. I won't be there for a few days. If y'all need me, just call my cell or page me," Braheem said.

"Where will you be at? You know Eric likes me to keep an eye on you," Edna said jokingly but she was very serious. "I'll be at this girl named Heaven. She has a place downtown and I'll be there for a few days," Braheem grinned.

"Heaven? Do she drive a silver Lexus LS," Edna said, shocked. "Yeah, that's her. Do you know her," Braheem asked. "No, not really. But the new girl Coffe I been seeing is Heaven's best friend. They both work down at the Platinum Club," Edna said. "Yeah, I saw her this morning when I was on my way out of there. What a small world," Braheem laughed.

"Don't say nothing, Edna, just keep this between us. Maybe we can both find out more about Heaven and Coffe," Braheem said. "I already know a little about Heaven. Coffe said she loves money," Edna said. "What woman doesn't," Josh interrupted, and they laughed at the undeniable fact.

"This morning Coffe said something about her and Heaven needing to go by a daycare. That some big money was involved," Edna said. "Yeah, Heaven said something about a daycare also. Maybe they're gonna buy one," Braheem said. "I have to meet up with Eric and then I have to go see the connect. Just call me later," Braheem said, rushing out the front door.

Chapter Thirty-Four
A ROSE AMONG THORNS II

Heaven's silver Lexus was parked right across the street from the *Westside-Roses Among Thorns Daycare Center*. Coffe sat inside listening to the radio while Heaven went into the building. Moments later, Heaven walked out of the building and got back into her car. She quickly pulled out of the parking space and drove down the street.

"Guess who runs the daycare and comes there every day after she gets out of school," Heaven smiled. "No, you can't be serious," Coffe grinned. "Dead serious! I asked the secretary at the front desk did she know Rose and she damn near ran down her entire resume. She said that Rose is usually there between three and five. "Are you ready to tell Tony, Jr.," Coffe said. "No, not yet. I'll wait a few more days," Heaven said. "Why? Let's just tell him and get it over with," Coffe said seriously.

Heaven looked into her girlfriend's worried eyes and said, "If we lead Tony, Jr. along for a few more days, I bet after I tell him I found Rose he'll give us even more," Heaven smiled. "You're playing with fire. You know he has a reputation for getting people who play him for a fool," Coffe said.

"Fuck his reputation! If he wants Rose, he has to pay," Heaven said.

Coffe sat back in the chair with her arms crossed. Playing around with Tony, Jr. was not a good idea but she knew Heaven was a smart girl. She was hopeful Heaven knew what she was doing.

Chapter Thirty-Five
A ROSE AMONG THORNS II

Northeast Philly...

Inside Braheem's private getaway home, he and Eric were talking.

"Are you sure it was eight people inside the house," Eric asked. "I'm positive. I counted them myself. We all waited down the street on our bikes, watching them go inside the house," Braheem said. "Well, the news is saying that only six bodies have been accounted for. Maybe they haven't found the other two," Eric said. "Or maybe two of them escaped," Braheem said.

"Stop stressing, Braheem, you know better than that. Just stay on your toes and keep your ears to the streets. As long as y'all did a clean job everything should be fine," Eric said. "Eric, I'm not worried about that. The job we did was flawless, no fingerprints and no witnesses. I'm worried about the two people who escaped. I ain't want none of those cowards to live," Braheem said, pacing across the room.

Eric walked over and gave Braheem a brotherly hug. He then picked up his briefcase and walked over to the door. "I have a few business meetings to take care of. If you need me, just call me," he said. "Eric, you know I don't like calling you about stuff like this. You're legit now. Look at you. Italian made suits, Gucci loafers, and your briefcase. You passed the game over to me," Braheem said.

"You're still my little cousin and I don't want anything to ever happen to you. So I'm here whenever you need me," Eric said sincerely.

Braheem watched as Eric walked out of the door and got into his Mercedes and drove off. After Eric left, he went down into the basement and started taking stacks of money from out of the washing machine. He placed what he needed inside of two black backpacks. Once the backpacks were filled with cash, Braheem walked out the house and got into his Navigator. He started to drive towards North Philly to meet his connect.

Lewisburg Prison...

Johnny Ray had just finished reading another letter that he received from his new attorney. The lawyer discussed more valuable information that could help him with his case. Johnny Ray was excited about the possibility of one day having his freedom back, and getting his life sentence overturned.

He decided that the only person he would share his good news with was Eric. Johnny Ray didn't want anyone else to get false hopes. Lying back on his bunk, Johnny Ray grabbed his Holy Bible and opened it up to Matthew 25- 35:36.

"For I was hungry and you gave me food; I was thirsty and you gave me drink; I was a stranger and you took me in; I was naked and you clothed me; I was in prison and you came to me."

Johnny Ray tearfully laid down his bible and thought about the last six years of his incarceration. He realized that he had to lose it all just to find himself. Prison offered up a lot of loses but on the other hand it had brought him a lot closer to God.

Johnny Ray felt a warm, comforting sensation move throughout his body. A feeling like he had never felt before. He lay back on his bunk and held onto the hope of a brighter tomorrow; and his chance at a future beyond the walls.

Chapter Thirty-Six
A ROSE AMONG THORNS II

Friday Evening
North Philly...

When Braheem walked into the house he sat the two backpacks down on the floor, and then two large Dominican men patted him down. After ensuring he wasn't strapped, one of the men walked in a back room. A few moments later the man returned with yet another fellow.

"Braheem, it's good to see you my friend. How's Eric doing," Jose said, walking up and shaking Braheem's hand. "He's doing fine, Jose," Braheem said. "Good, good. Eric is a very good friend of mine. Me and him go back a long way," Jose smiled. "Nino, Romero, leave us." Jose ordered.

The two men quickly walked out of the room. "I've been watching and reading the news lately. I see that there's a lot of killings going on in West and Southwest Philly," Jose said, looking Braheem straight in the eyes. "You know that no one makes money when there is so much violence and killings going on," Jose said. "Is there something that I need to know? Maybe I can help..." Jose said, walking over to a chair and sitting down.

"No, I'm fine, everything is under control. My crew will handle it," Braheem said.

Jose shook his head. "Braheem, you remind me a lot of your cousin, Eric. I can see the determination in your eyes. The same determination

Eric had. The only difference between y'all is your violent nature. Eric thinks before he moves while you move before you think," Jose said, with his Spanglish accent.

"I hope you're right and this little problem you're having can be taken care of," he said. "I'll take care of everything, Jose, you got my word on that," Braheem said seriously.

"Is that everything you owe me," Jose said, pointing at the two backpacks on the floor. "Yeah, it's two hundred and fifty thousand," Braheem said, picking up the backpacks and sitting them by Jose's feet.

"Good, I'll make sure Raul takes care of you," Jose said, as he opened up one of the backpacks and looked inside. "You're a good man, Braheem. You and Eric did a big favor for me down Miami and I'll never forget that. But all I'm asking is for you to think before you make moves and to keep playing the background. Often it's better to be heard than seen," Jose said, standing up from his chair.

One of the men walked back into the room and whispered something into Jose's ear, as he smiled and replied "Good."

Jose walked over to Braheem and shook his hand. "Tell Eric I asked about him. When you get in your truck everything you need is already inside for you. I hope the next time we meet your little problem is fixed. You're making me nervous, my friend, and I don't like being nervous. I hope you understand," Jose said. "I do," Braheem said, walking out the door.

When Braheem got into his truck, he looked at the large green duffle bag and smiled. Then he started up his truck and drove away while playing his favorite rap group I.C.H.

Late Friday Night...

"Rose, I miss him so much," Joyce cried into the phone. "This shit is driving me crazy! I'm starting to lose my hair, weight, and I can't even sleep at night without crying myself to sleep," Joyce said. "Joyce, I told you that you can't keep jumping to conclusions. And you just can't accuse Braheem of cheating on you if you're not totally sure. I told you that you were gonna run him away acting like that. He's young, and young men like Braheem don't like to feel locked down," Rose said.

"Eric did say he spoke with Braheem earlier, but he doesn't know when he's coming back home. My advice to you is to stop calling his cell phone and pager and just wait for Braheem to come back home," she said.

"Rose, I have something to tell you," Joyce said. "What is it," she asked. "I missed my period and I'm pregnant," Joyce said. "What! I thought you were on birth control," Rose snapped. "I stopped taking my pills because they made me feel so sick," Joyce said.

"Do Braheem know you're pregnant," Rose asked. "No, nobody knows except you. And I don't want you to tell anybody, not even Eric. I want to be the first person to tell Braheem that he's gonna be a father," Joyce said. "Alright. I won't say a word... Congratulations," Rose said excitingly. She wasn't sure if being pregnant was the best thing for her friend but she was always going to support her.

"Thanks, Rose, now all I need is my man back home so I can tell him the good news," Joyce said, lying back on the bed while rubbing her stomach.

Inside Heaven's Condominium...

"Yes! Oh, yes! Keep it right there!!! I'm cuming again," Heaven shouted, as Braheem had her body bent over the bed; fucking her from behind.

Braheem walked Heaven over to the large eight-foot wall mirror.

"Put your hands on the mirror," he ordered. She did as she was told, facing the mirror and placing her hands on it. "Spread your legs," he said. Once again Heaven did as she was told. Braheem was a control freak and it had only turned her on more.

Braheem walked behind Heaven and slid his hard dick inside her wet pussy. "Oohhh!!" she moaned out in pure pleasure. Braheem began treating her pussy with long, thunderous strokes. In and out of Heaven's pussy he went, often twirling his dick around to hit all of her spots.

"Look in the mirror. I want you to watch me tear this pussy up," he grunted loudly. Heaven watched Braheem sex her through the large wall mirror. She moaned, grunted and begged for more. Heaven's body started trembling as a wonderful orgasm swept through her entire body.

This young man was giving her all the loving she desired and if he kept at it, it wouldn't be long before she was turned out; if she wasn't already.

Chapter Thirty-Seven
A ROSE AMONG THORNS II

When the loud explosion went off, Willie and Sanchez were knocked to the kitchen floor. The impact from the hand grenade was that strong. Luckily they had been inside the kitchen when the grenade was thrown through the front window, because they survived while everyone else was dead. The two of them only had a few minor bruises and were able to make it out the back door. They rushed down a back alley and quickly disappeared into the darkness of the night.

Willie and Sanchez had underestimated Braheem and his crew; and now six of Willie's top street workers had to pay for it with their young lives. The next day, Willie and Sanchez packed all of their possessions and moved together in a West Philly apartment. They also purchased a new tinted Land Cruiser to get around in. Willie needed time to regroup and get himself together. He still couldn't believe that six of his men were dead, including his top lieutenant Lance. He knew he had to lay low until things had settled down.

The cops and Feds were all over the streets, searching for answers to their many questions. Willie knew that Braheem was behind everything. He also learned that J.T. had been found dead behind the Elmwood Roller Rink with the words, "Never trust your friends." inscribed on his body. Now Willie knew exactly who the traitor inside of his crew was.

But J.T. was dead and it was too late to do anything to him.

Willie and Sanchez stayed in during the day and cruised through the streets at night. The war was far from over. It was just the beginning. Sanchez couldn't believe that his best friend and partner in crime was dead. He and Lance had been friends for forever and now he was gone. For two days Sanchez cried as he remembered his comrade. Revenge lingered inside his soul and Sanchez couldn't wait to release his anger on someone. Sanchez was angry but very cautious. In the daytime he slept with his AK-47 right next to him.

At night he cruised around with Willie hoping to find a few victims to inflict his pain on. Tonight Willie and Sanchez had a special visit to make and both men were looking forward to it. Someone was going to pay severely.

"You ready for tonight," Willie said, smoking on his blunt, while reading The Philadelphia Daily News paper. "Yeah, this will calm me down a little, at least until we really get the ones I want," Sanchez said, sitting on the sofa wiping his AK-47 down with a towel. "Don't worry, Sanchez, their time will come shortly. Let's just get one duck at a time," Willie said. "Just like they did us, they won't even know what hit 'em," he laughed.

Chapter Thirty-Eight
A ROSE AMONG THORNS II

Saturday Afternoon
Lewisburg Federal Prison...

The large visiting room was packed with people from wall to wall. Every table was occupied with three or four people sitting down at each tabletop. Men, women and children all came to visit their incarcerated loved ones. A few unarmed COs were posted throughout the large visiting room, trying their best to keep an eye on all of the people around them.

Johnny Ray sat next to his wife, their hands clutched tightly under the table; and seated directly across from them was Eric and Rose. Rose's two younger brothers were inside the children's playroom with a handful of other children playing with board games and toys. They had been there for over an hour.

While everyone sat around talking, Eric stood up to go to the vending machine. When he got there, Eric noticed a familiar face staring at him. It was the head CO of the visiting room. The tall, slim, dark-skinned man smilingly approached.

"Hey, Eric, you don't remember me," he said. "No, I'm sorry. Your face looks familiar though," Eric said. "Doug Little. I moved in one of your houses a few months ago," he said. Eric thought for a few seconds as he began to remember.

"Oh yeah, you and your wife and your two little girls, the Little's," Eric said, shaking the man's hand. "So this is where you work," Eric asked. "Yeah, six years next month. I just got visiting room duty a few weeks ago. I'm in charge up here for the entire quarter," Doug said, feeling proud of himself.

"I saw you over there with Johnny Ray. He's a good man. Stays to himself, does a lot of reading of his Bible and just works out. I never had one problem with him," Doug said. "Yeah, that's my fiancé's father," Eric said.

"So you're in charge of all the other COs that work in here," Eric asked. "Yup. I'm usually in the back monitoring the video screens or doing paperwork," Doug said.

Eric stood there and looked around the large room of boisterous people. Suddenly he had an idea. Why not? He thought.

"Doug, how much is your monthly payment on your house," Eric asked. Unsure of why Eric had asked him, but intrigued he answered, "You charge us six-hundred and fifty dollars."
"How would you like to keep that this month for a small favor," Eric asked.

Doug smiled and so did Eric.
"The wife would love that," Doug said. "Do you know what I need you to do for me," Eric said. "Don't you worry, Eric. I've done it plenty of times already. I'll tell my men to look the other way for thirty minutes," Doug said as he walked away.

Eric grabbed his four bags of chips and rushed back to the table.

"Baby, you know that guy," Rose asked.

117

"Yeah, he lives in one of our houses," Eric smiled.

Eric leaned over and whispered in Johnny Ray's ear. "Are you serious," he said excitingly. "You got thirty minutes," Eric said, with a serious expression on his face.

Johnny Ray quickly stood up and walked over by the CO's work station. A few moments later, a white CO walked over to the table and asked his wife to follow him.

"What's wrong," she said, in a scared voice. "Ma'am, can you just follow me please. It has something to do with your husband," the CO said. She stood up from the table and followed the CO through the crowded visiting room.

"What's going on," Rose said, confused and upset. "Eric, what happened with you and that CO," Rose asked. Eric grabbed Rose's hands and looked into her worried eyes. "Baby, everything is fine," he said calmly. "No... you really didn't just do that," Rose smiled. "Yes, I did! I think six plus years is a long enough time for a man to go without no loving," Eric laughed. "Don't you? You can barely go without it for six hours," he continued. "Shut up, boy," Rose said, playfully pushing Eric's shoulder.

"I ain't that bad," she said. "Tell it to somebody else. I'm the one who sleeps in bed with you every night," Eric said, leaning over and giving Rose a kiss on the lips. "Just wait till tonight," Rose said.

Inside a small supply closet that was next to the CO's locker room, Johnny Ray and his wife were at each other like two lost lovers who finally reunited after many years of separation. Johnny Ray had his wife's dress lifted up and began making love to her from behind.

"The only thing that separates us is time, my love. And soon time will be up," he whispered softly into his wife's ear.

The two reunited lovers were lost in a world of sensual pleasure. Thirty minutes later, Johnny Ray and his wife walked up to the table, smiling, and holding hands. Rose and Eric smiled, seeing the glow on both of their satisfied faces.

"Y'all look like two teenagers in love," Rose said. "And that's just how I feel," Rose's mother said, leaning over and quickly kissing Johnny Ray's lips. "Hey, I feel about twenty years younger myself!" Johnny Ray said, as everyone burst out laughing.

As the visitation came to a close Johnny Ray had asked the ladies to go to the restroom so he could speak to Eric. He told him about the good news he had received from his new lawyer and made Eric promise to keep the news between the two men.

"Eric thanks for everything," Johnny Ray said, shaking his hand and giving him a hug. "I can't thank you enough for all that you have done for my family," Johnny Ray said, as the tears welled up in his eyes. "You're welcome, Johnny Ray. For my Rose I'll do anything to make her happy," Eric said, reaching out and grabbing Rose's hand as she walked up beside him.

Together they all stood and shared one long group hug. Johnny Ray looked into Rose's watery eyes and said, "You know how to pick 'em."
"I learned from the best, never be less than a queen," Rose said, as the tears started to fall down her face.

Johnny Ray tearfully watched as his family walked out of the visiting room. He was the last prisoner to be searched before returning back to his cell.

"Did you enjoy yourself," Doug asked him. "I think you already know the answer to that question, CO," Johnny Ray said as a smile as big a life came upon his face.

Inside his cell, Johnny Ray laid across his bunk holding his bible. "Thank you, God, thank you," he whispered softly.

Chapter Thirty-Nine
A ROSE AMONG THORNS II

Saturday Night
Inside Heaven's Condominium...

"Whose pussy is this!!! Tell me whose pussy is this," Braheem yelled, as he had Heaven spread out on the bed with her long legs wrapped around his broad shoulders. "Yours!!! Yours!!!! Oohhh! Fuck me! Fuck me harder, Braheem!!!" Heaven screamed out, as her pussy clenched tighter before another powerful orgasm swept through her shuddering body.

Quickly, Braheem turned Heaven around onto her stomach. They both breathed deeply and heavily, and the aroma of sex filled the air.

"Do you want more," he yelled out.
"Yes! Yes, I want it," Heaven begged. "I said do you want it," Braheem asked again with more authority. "Yes! Yes! Yes! I want it! Please give it to me!!!" Heaven begged louder.

Braheem reached over and grabbed a handful of Heaven's long black hair. After a long, deep breath, Braheem slowly slid his hard dick inside of Heaven's tight asshole. Heaven was loving this rim-shot. She felt like he was pleasing a part of her body that most men had no clue how to satisfy. He was gentle but firm; enough to penetrate her deeply enough to give her another orgasm. She was officially turned out.

Chapter Forty
A ROSE AMONG THORNS II

Willie and Sanchez had been sitting inside the vehicle for fifteen minutes until Willie saw it was time to make a move. "Grab your gun. It's time," Willie said, getting out of the truck. Sanchez left his AK in the truck and got out but he had his loaded Glock in hand.

They walked up to the small row home and knocked on the door. A female looked out the front window and saw who it was. Then she quickly ran and opened the door.

"Willie, Sanchez, it's good to see y'all. J.T.'s funeral is next week at the..." When she saw the gun in Willie's hand, she cut her sentence short. Her eyes were now filled with fear. Keisha Bradly was J.T.'s pregnant girlfriend. She was three months pregnant with their second child. J.T., Keisha and their five-year-old son, all lived with Keisha's elderly mother.

Willie quickly grabbed Keisha by the throat and pointed his 9mm between her eyes. "Blame this on that no-good traitor you loved," Willie said, squeezing the trigger one time. POW!!! Keisha's body collapsed onto the hard floor. She moaned heavily as life escaped from her body.

Sanchez quickly ran upstairs into her mother's bedroom. She was still sleeping in bed when he walked up to her and pointed the gun at her head.

"Sweet dreams, Grandma," he said, shooting her once in the head. When he ran out of the bedroom, Jr. was walking down the hallway. He had been awakened by the loud gunshot.

"Who you," the child asked, frightened. Sanchez grabbed Jr. by his shirt and dragged the boy back into his bedroom. Without any hesitation, he shot Jr. twice in the head. His small body fell to the floor. And now just like his mother and father, his unborn sibling and his grandmother, he was dead.

Willie and Sanchez walked out of the house and quickly pulled off down the dark street.

"Feel better," Willie asked. "Just a little," Sanchez said. "Don't worry. Braheem, Edna and Josh will all get theirs. Remember, one duck at a time," Willie said, driving by Bartram High School.

"One duck at a time until I've got their goose," Willie said.

Chapter Forty-One
A ROSE AMONG THORNS II

Monday Morning...

Joyce sat on the sofa staring at pictures of her and Braheem. She hadn't seen or heard from Braheem since their argument on Thursday night. Her eyes were bloodshot red as the tears steadily fell upon her face. For four days she had been crying nonstop and longing the return and touch of her man. As Joyce sat on the sofa filled with anguish she heard the sounds of a car pulling up.

Quickly she ran over to the window and looked through the curtains. Joyce unlocked the front door and sat back on the sofa, but she was filled with disappointment because the visitor was not who she desired. Seconds later, Rose walked through the front door.

The first thing Rose noticed was the depressing look on Joyce's face. Her long hair, which was usually well-kept, was now all over the place and dark bags were forming under her worried eyes. Rose walked over and sat beside her friend on the sofa. She reached out and hugged Joyce in her comforting and love-filled arms.

"Rose, I miss my man," Joyce cried out. "Why won't he call me or come back home? Why," she said, wiping the tears from her eyes. For a few moments, Rose was speechless. She thought about how she would feel if she was in Joyce's shoes and

Eric had left her. Just the thought of Eric not being in their bed every night gave her a scare.

"Something just ain't right. I can feel it. He got somebody else," Joyce cried. "Joyce, Braheem loves you. There's no one out there that can take him from you. He'll be back home," Rose said. "When? When, Rose? I'm around here pregnant and stressing my ass off. When," Joyce yelled out.

"When the moment is right, Joyce," Rose said softly. "I took off from school today because you have to get out of this house. So go get dressed. We're going to pamper ourselves today," Rose said. "I don't want to hear nothing... just get in the shower and get dressed. I have a few hours before I have to be at the daycare so hurry up," Rose said, grabbing Joyce's arm and walking her upstairs.

"Ryan is over your mother's so you have some time. Let's get out for a few hours and get you and that baby some fresh air," Rose said, softly pushing Joyce inside the bathroom and closing the door. "I'll pick you out something to wear," Rose continued, walking into the bedroom and going into Joyce's closet.

While Joyce was showering, Rose picked out a nice outfit and laid it across the bed. Then she took out her cell phone and called Eric.

"Hello, my love...you've gotta make it fast. I'm on my way to a meeting with my lawyer," Eric said into the phone. "I'm over here with Joyce. She's in the bathroom taking a shower. Can you please talk to Braheem, please," Rose asked desperately. "Baby, I told you already, Braheem will come home when he's ready. You know I don't like getting involved in other people's relationship. Just trust me, they'll work it out," Eric said.

Rose wasn't convinced and now as she thought about her friend's unfortunate situation she had some worries of her own.

"I want you to promise me something," Rose said. "Anything," Eric said. "Promise me you'll never treat me like he does Joyce. Don't ever leave me alone guessing where you are," Rose said in all seriousness.

Eric laughed into the phone causing Rose to become frustrated and she said, "Eric, I'm serious." He could sense her worries were real but knew she had nothing to worry about. "I promise you that I'll never treat you like that. We are two different men with two different styles. Now I love you and I have to go. Goodbye," Eric said, as he hung up knowing he would never want to give up his Rose.

Chapter Forty-Two
A ROSE AMONG THORNS II

"Tonight we're going out man-hunting until we find them bitch-ass niggas," Willie said, eating a bowl of Cap'n Crunch cereal. "My money is all fucked up! I gotta get those bastards for what they did to our crew," Willie vented.

"I'm ready now," Sanchez yelled from the couch. "No, we gonna stick to the plan and keep searching for them at night. Sooner or later they'll have to show their faces and when they do, we'll take them right the fuck off," Willie laughed.

"I want them to hurt like we did," Sanchez said. "Don't worry, they will. When you play in this game everyone gets hurts sooner or later. Someone told me a long time ago that thugs, hustlers and gangsters got a lot of tears inside of them just waiting to be released," Willie said, pouring himself another bowl of cereal. Sanchez stared at him not sure of what his point was exactly. He didn't feel any fear and didn't have any tears bundled up inside. He continued to listen but still was a bit lost. All he wanted was revenge.

"Don't worry, Sanchez, I see the worry in your eyes but we will fix this situation real soon."

Chapter Forty-Three
A ROSE AMONG THORNS II

After Joyce had taken a shower and gotten dressed, the duo walked downstairs. Before Rose opened the front door, Joyce grabbed her arm.

"Hold up," Joyce said. "What is it, Joyce," Rose said, looking into her eyes. "Before we leave can you please say one of your poems for me? Please," Joyce pleaded. "Come on Joyce, not right now," Rose said, rushing to get out of the door. "Please, Rose, you know your poems always cheer me up," Joyce said. "Okay, Joyce, but just one," Rose said.

Rose thought for a moment about which one of her many poems she should recite.

"Okay, here go one. It's called, *Behind My Tears*," Rose said.

Behind my tears is the secret to my perpetual happiness, waiting to be released from the depths of my crying soul
Behind my tears is an Island called Love, that is so hard to find and it's surrounded by an ocean of pain and heartache
The sun rarely shines and when it does most times there's no one to share it with
Behind my tears is too many years of confusion and too many joys built on illusion
Behind my tears are too many chances and too many meaningless romances
Behind my tears is lust, sex and so many lies...

And the more I try to wipe my tears away, the more they pain and watery misery falls from my eyes.

"Rose, that is just beautiful," Joyce said, as she stood wiping her tears away. "Thank you, Joyce. "Now can we go out and enjoy ourselves," Rose said, grabbing Joyce's hand and walking out of the front door.

Together they got inside of Rose's brand new red BMW.

"How about we hit up the Cherry Hill Mall and then we can go downtown and get us a pedicure," Rose said, starting her car up and pulling out of the parking space. "I thought you had to be at the daycare this afternoon," Joyce said, fixing her makeup in the mirror. "Don't worry. We got enough time," Rose said, switching gears and speeding away.

Chapter Forty-Four
A ROSE AMONG THORNS II

After Braheem had gotten Edna's emergency call, he quickly got out of Heaven's bed and put on his clothes.

"Baby, where are you rushing off to," Heaven said, seeing the serious expression plastered on Braheem's face. "I have to meet somebody," Braheem said, putting on his shirt. "Anyway I thought you had to go talk to your boss about something this morning," Braheem said, as he tied up his Timberland boots. "I do but that's not for a few more hours. It's not even twelve yet," Heaven said, looking over at the wall clock.

"Is Coffe home," he asked. "Yeah, I heard her come in about twenty minutes ago," Braheem said. Heaven slyly pulled the covers to the side of the bed and exposed her beautiful naked brown body. She stood up from the bed and walked over to Braheem.

"I know your ass don't want no more," Braheem said. "No, not after last night. My body needs a rest for a few hours. Maybe tonight," Heaven said, smilingly wrapping her arms around his waist. "What time will you be here tonight," Heaven said softly. "As soon as I finish with my business," Braheem said. "And what time will that be," Heaven questioned.

Braheem gave Heaven an uneasy look. "I'm sorry, baby, I'll just see you when you get here," she said, kissing his lips. Heaven grabbed her robe and followed Braheem into the living room. Coffe was sitting on the sofa when they entered.

"Oh, they do come up for air... so y'all are human," Coffe jokingly said. "Are we going to talk to our buddy today about the daycare situation," Coffe asked Heaven, as she walked Braheem over to the front door.

"Yeah, as soon as I get cleaned up and dressed," Heaven said. "What is all this daycare stuff y'all keep talking about," Braheem asked.
"It's nothing. We just doing a favor for a friend," Heaven said.

After Braheem had given Heaven a kiss and a hug, she stood in the doorway and watched as he got inside of his Navigator and quickly sped off. When she closed the door and turned around, Coffe was staring at her with both arms crossed and a big smile on her face.

"Damn, girl, I thought I was strung out. He got you hooked," Coffe laughed. Heaven smiled and walked over and sat down on the sofa beside her.

"Don't get it confused or twisted, Coffe. Braheem is fine, paid and he fucks better than any man I ever had but the only thing that got Heaven strung out is dead old white men on green and white paper," Heaven said, as they gave each other a high five. "I'm about to get washed up and dressed so we can go talk to Tony, Jr.," Heaven said.

Coffe watched as Heaven stood up from the sofa and walked back into her bedroom.

Chapter Forty-Five
A ROSE AMONG THORNS II

Korman Suites Apartments
Southwest Philly...

When Braheem arrived at Edna's apartment Josh had already been inside waiting.

"What's the problem now," Braheem said, walking through the door and slamming it behind him. "The news released the six names of the men who were killed inside the house and Willie and Sanchez names weren't two of them," Edna said. "Damn!!! Out of all the men inside that house how did those two escape," Braheem said.

"That ain't all Braheem," Josh said nervously. "What else, Braheem said, pacing the floor.
"One of my workers swears he saw two people driving around Saturday night in a Land Cruiser that look just like Willie and Sanchez," Josh said.
"So them two niggas is plotting, huh," Braheem snapped.

"That's not all, there's more," Edna said.
"Of course there is," Braheem said. "Saturday night someone murdered J.T.'s pregnant girlfriend, his son and his girlfriend's mom. They found them yesterday morning," Edna said. "That's Willie and Sanchez work! They retaliated on J.T.'s family because he was a fuckin traitor. He knew what I meant when I wrote that shit on J.T.'s body. Damn, I'm the cause of these people's death..."

Braheem was instantly filled with an overwhelming feeling of grief. Edna and Josh watched as Braheem sat down on the sofa with his head hung low to the floor. Edna walked over and sat beside him.

"Braheem, you can't blame yourself for what happened to J.T.'s family. What you did to J.T. can't account for what Willie and Sanchez did to J.T.'s family. They didn't have to kill his family. They chose to do that and you don't have anything to do with that," Edna said, doing her best to console her friend.

"So what's next," Josh said. "I already told my boys to be on point," he continued. Edna stood up and walked into the back room. When she walked back out she was carrying a large brown suitcase in her hand.

"Last night and this morning, me and Josh picked up the rest of the money that was owed. This is four-hundred thousand," Edna said, passing the suitcase to Braheem. "Inside are two new loaded 9mm. Make sure you keep them on you at all times... Josh and I got ours. I'll keep my eyes and ears open for Willie and Sanchez but I need you to be safe," Edna said seriously.

Braheem stood up and took the suitcase as he walked over to the door.

"How is Levi doing," Braheem asked, trying to get back focused. "Levi is fine. We drove up to see him on Saturday. He's still rehabbing that leg but the doc said he won't be ready for at least another month or so," Josh said. "I've been running his post for him and he'll be good until he's able to get back on his feet," he continued.

Braheem walked over and gave Edna and Josh both a brotherly hug.

"If you need me, I'll be over Heaven's tonight," he said, walking out the door with the suitcase in his right hand; and the guilt of the lost lives in the other.

A Few Hours Later...

After Rose and Joyce finished shopping at the mall, they drove downtown and got themselves manicures, facials and pedicures. Being out with Rose was beneficial for Joyce; she surely needed the fresh air. Rose did a wonderful job consoling her friend. She promised to always lend her shoulder whenever her girlfriend needed someone to lean on; and Joyce offered her the same support. Their friendship had grown much stronger since their initial bonding when they both lived at the West Park Housing Projects.

After pampering themselves, Rose dropped Joyce back off at home and told her that she would call later to check up on her. Joyce stood in the doorway holding all of her shopping bags, as she waved goodbye to her dear friend.

When Joyce walked inside of her beautiful, calm home, she felt so much better. Once again, Rose had come to her rescue and she was forever grateful to have a true sister-friend.

Chapter Forty-Six
A ROSE AMONG THORNS II

Inside the Platinum Club Parking Lot...

"Coffe, wait right here, I'll be right back," Heaven said. "You sure you don't want me to go inside with you," Coffe asked. "No, I'm fine; I want to talk to Tony, Jr. alone. I got this... Just chill," Heaven said, getting out of the car and walking up to the back door entrance. Coffe watched Heaven go into the building, and she nervously and anxiously waited for her girlfriend to return.

Heaven walked upstairs to Tony, Jr.'s private office. His two bodyguards were standing outside the door.

"Tell Tony, Jr. I need to see him," Heaven said. Rocko knocked on the door and then walked inside. Tony, Jr. was sitting on the edge of his desk watching a beautiful, young Spanish woman perform for him. He was auditioning the lovely female for a new opening he had at the club.

"What is it, Rocko," Tony, Jr. said, sounding disturbed. "Boss, Heaven is at the door. She said she needs to see you," Rocko said, as the bass in his voice increased. Tony, Jr. stood up and walked over to the attractive Spanish female.

"Sophia that was a wonderful job. I have your phone number and so far you're the front runner for the opening I have. I'll let you know in a few days if you got the job. I have a few more women to look at but I wish you the best," he said to the sexy young beauty. "Thank you so much. When Coffe told me about the opening I just wanted to jump on it fast. If I get the job I promise you won't be disappointed," Sophia said, as she grabbed her bra and thong from off the floor, and quickly placed them on before walking out of the office.

"Alright, Rocco, tell Heaven to come in," Tony, Jr. said, folding his arms across his chest. Heaven walked into the office and shut the door behind her.

"I hope you have some good news," Tony, Jr. said. "Great news," Heaven said, with a bright grin on her face. "But before I give it to you, Tony, Jr., we need to discuss a few things," she said. "What," he demanded. "Money," Heaven said.

Northeast Philly...

When Braheem pulled up in front of his house he was surprised to see Eric's Mercedes Benz parked out front. Braheem grabbed the suitcase and walked inside. Eric was sitting on the sofa reading the Daily Newspaper.

"Did you read this," Eric said, passing Braheem the paper. Braheem sat down the suitcase and read the front page of the newspaper. The headline read: *Southwest Family Brutally Massacred.* Braheem quickly passed the paper back to Eric.

"I already know. Edna and Josh told me about this earlier today," Braheem said, taking a seat on the sofa beside Eric. "Do you also know that Willie and Sanchez didn't die in that house bombing," Eric said.

"Yeah, they told me that too," Braheem said. "So you're on your job then, huh," Eric asked, looking concerned and unsure if Braheem was on his A-game.

"Always. You taught me to stay on point," Braheem said. "So what's up with you and Joyce," Eric said, changing the subject. "Eric, please don't start on that. Me and Joyce will be fine," Braheem said. "Not if you keep fucking Heaven y'all won't be," Eric said. "How do you know about Heaven," Braheem questioned. "Edna told me. You didn't think she would," Eric said. "Well, it's cool. Me and Heaven is just friends. I mean the sex is good but I don't love her. I love Joyce," he said.

"Sometimes just sex can evolve into much deeper feelings and more trouble down the road if you're not careful," Eric said, waiting for Braheem's response. "Like I said, the sex is good and Heaven is a very attractive female but Joyce is and will always be the love of my life," Braheem said.

Eric reached out and put his hand on Braheem's shoulder.

"Good answer. Just remember you have a good woman at home who loves the ground you walk on. At the same time don't lead Heaven on. Be up front with her so she will understand where she stands," Eric said. "I did already. She knows about my relationship. We are just having a good time," Braheem said. "Good, good, good, that's great," Eric smiled.

"One last thing. How are you gonna handle this Willie and Sanchez situation? You know they are looking for you and your crew," Eric said.

"I know they are. Just like I know they murdered J.T.'s family inside that house. Don't worry, Eric, we'll find them soon. Willie can't fight a war without money or a crew to help him," Braheem laughed.

"Just remember this always, Braheem. When a man is determined to do something and he has his mind set on doing it, he won't need a crew. He'll do it himself," Eric said as he stood up from the sofa. "Think about that and I'll call you later," Eric said, shaking Braheem's hand and walking out the door.

Inside the Platinum Club...

"What do you mean more money," Tony, Jr. yelled out. "You ain't show me shit yet," Heaven said. "I told you that I got all the info on Rose you will need. Now if you want it I need to know about this money," Heaven said.

Tony, Jr. smiled and walked over to his desk. He reached under his desk and took out a black leather sports bag. "How much money you talking about Heaven," he said, as he unzipped the bag.

"I want thirty-five thousand and I'll give you all I got," she said. Tony, Jr. looked into Heaven's greedy eyes. "You play hard Heaven" he said. "The only way to play is hard," Heaven said.

Tony, Jr. reached into the bag and started taking out stacks of money. He sat seven stacks of five-thousand on top of each other.

"Here's your thirty-five thousand but first I'm gonna need the info on Rose," Tony, Jr. said.

"Come on, do I look that stupid? First let me take the money outside to my car and you can follow me outside; but only you. Once I'm safely inside I'll pass you the info I have on Rose," Heaven said. "What, you don't trust me," Tony, Jr. smiled. "I don't trust my own mother when money is involved," Heaven said. "Now do you want the info on Rose or not? If you want it, you'll find her today," Heaven said.

"Today," Tony, Jr. said excitingly. "That's right. I have information on where she'll be at between 3 and 5 o'clock today," Heaven said. "It's your call," she continued. "Okay, you win, Heaven," Tony, Jr. said, picking up the money and passing it to Heaven.

Heaven lifted up her blouse and placed the seven stacks inside her tight-fitted waistline of her jeans. She pulled her blouse back down and said, "Now follow me."

When they walked out of the office, Tony, Jr. told his two bodyguards not to follow him. They both did as they were told and watched as he and Heaven walked down the stairs and went outside. When they walked over to Heaven's car, they saw Coffe, who was inside listening to the radio. Heaven quickly got inside the car and shut the door. She rolled down the window while Tony, Jr. waited outside the car. Heaven reached down into her bra and passed Tony, Jr. a folded white piece of paper.

"That's where Rose works at. She's the manager of the place and she's always there between three and five. If I'm wrong, which I'm not, I'll give you back every single penny," Heaven said.

"So you had the info on you the whole time, huh," he said, as he giggled. "Better safe than sorry… ain't that what they say," Heaven said.

Tony, Jr. unfolded the piece of paper and looked at the address. "She works at a daycare center, huh," he said. "Yeah, the same daycare center that her fiancé owns. I'll see you on Wednesday night when my shift starts. It was nice doing business with you but now I must say Goodbye," Heaven said, rolling up the window and driving away.

Tony, Jr. folded up the piece of paper and walked back into the club.

Chapter Forty-Seven
A ROSE AMONG THORNS II

When Joyce heard someone knocking at the door, she jumped off the sofa and ran over to the door. Only her family and true friends were allowed at her house, so she knew it had to be one or the other. Once she saw who it was she quickly opened the door.

"Eric," Joyce said, giving him a long, warm hug. "I've missed you," Joyce said, shutting the door behind him. They walked over and sat down on the sofa. "What's up, Lil Sis," Eric asked. "Not much. Me and Ryan is good. My mom and my two sisters are cool too. They all miss you," Joyce said.
"I know. I've been real busy lately. I have to make it over there soon and check up on them. I sent your father some money too. They're going to hold him for a few months," Eric said.

"I know, he called me the other day and told me you sent him another stack," Joyce said smilingly, grabbing Eric's hands. "Look at you all dressed up looking like one of those models in VIBE. I hear you buying up all the property you can get your hands on. I'm so proud of you, Eric, especially all that you're doing for Mike. He would be so proud of you if he was still alive," Joyce said, as the reality of his passing made her a bit sad.

Eric reached over and hugged Joyce.
"I'm sure Mike's somewhere smiling down on both of us," Eric said, feeling and understanding her pain.

"So tell me. What's going on with you and Rose? When is the wedding," Joyce said, changing the sensitive subject. "Next 4th of July," Eric said. "On y'all birthday," Joyce said excitingly.

"Yup. Rose will be finished with her degree and I should have five more daycare centers up and running all throughout the city," Eric said enthusiastically.

"I want you to tell me what's going on with you and Braheem," Eric said. Joyce's happy expression quickly changed. "I don't know, Eric. I love Braheem and I'm sure he feels the same way but we have so many problems," Joyce said sadly.

"I want you to stay strong, Joyce, and hang in there. Braheem is young but he loves you. He knows he has a good thing in you. Y'all two have been through a lot together…and I know love, faith, and trust will keep ya'll on the right path," Eric said.

"Eric, I know he's sleeping with other women and I can't lie, it bothers me a lot," Joyce said, letting the tears run down her face. "I'm a hundred percent faithful to him. I don't even look at other man, Eric. So many men approach me on a daily but I don't care how cute they are or how paid they are, all I want in my life is my man," Joyce cried. "Eric, do you think Braheem and Edna are sleeping around? He says it's all business but look at Edna, she's very pretty and they're always together. How can a man be around an attractive woman like Edna all day and not have sex with her," Joyce said.

Eric looked deep into Joyce's watery eyes and asked, "Do you trust me?" She quickly responded, "Yes," she said. "Then listen to me. Braheem and

Edna's relationship is nothing more than business. She's his right hand, and his eyes and the ears that Braheem desperately needs on them streets. I introduced Edna to Braheem because I knew she would make sure he was safe out there. Joyce, I'm not gonna sit here and tell you that Braheem is a saint, none of us are. But I will tell you this, Lil Sis, if you want your man to change his ways, you must first change yours. That spoiled, jealous attitude of yours has got to go. Stop thinking your pretty face and nice body can get you everything you want.

Braheem loves you for who you are. He has always had a crush on you and that crush turned into love. I told you all about hustlers. Hustlers live a fast, dangerous lifestyle. We need our women to be our backbones, not our adversaries. A man cannot win the war alone, Joyce; he needs his queen to be there for him; holding that extra ammunition whenever he runs out. You knew what you were getting involved in once you accepted Braheem into your life. The only thing that will change him is your love for him, not sex or your threats," Eric said.

Joyce sat in total silence. She knew how close they were and his words were true. As her tears fell from her face, she reached over and gave Eric a long hug.

"Thank you, Eric! Thank you so much for being here for me," she said. "I'm always here for you, Lil Sis, always. We all we got," Eric said, as a tear fell from one of his eyes.

Inside the Platinum Club...

"The Roses Among Thorns Daycare Center, huh," Tony, Jr. thought to himself. The search for his father's murderer had finally come to an end. In his heart he believed Rose was responsible and he wanted her to pay.

"I want y'all to go to that daycare and find her," Tony, Jr. said to his two guards, as he passed the piece of paper to Rocko. "Y'all already have her photo so y'all know what this bitch looks like," he continued. "Boss, if we find her do you want us to take care of her today," Knuckles asked. "When y'all find her get rid of her ass! I don't want to miss out on the chance of killing this bitch! I've waited too long to find this woman...and I don't care if she's surrounded by any goddamn kids either. If y'all see her, get rid of her and anyone else that's in the way," Tony, Jr. said.

"And don't fuck this up! My father's dead because of this bitch! She set him up. I know her type. She's nothing but an innocent looking black slut that goes around manipulating people who fall for her beauty! Well, she might've gotten away with it with my father but it will never happen with me! Kill that bitch," he continued.

Rocko and Knuckles both looked at their boss as devious intentions filled their eyes.

"Don't worry Boss, we'll handle this," Rocko said, as he and Knuckles walked out of the office leaving Tony, Jr. all alone with his impending feelings that he would finally have his revenge.

Chapter Forty-Eight
A ROSE AMONG THORNS II

43rd & Pennsgrove Street
West Philly...

Inside one of Braheem's stash houses, Edna and Josh stood around with five young men. Next to Edna's leg was a dark green army duffle bag with ten kilos of cocaine inside. Edna reached down inside the bag and passed each of them two kilos a piece.

"I want 19.5 for each one when y'all bring me back mine. No ones, fives or tens. By now y'all all know that Willie and Sanchez are still alive, so please don't get caught slipping," Edna said, shaking everybody's hand and walking out of the front door with Josh closely behind her. The five men stood out front watching Edna and Josh get inside the blue Nissan Maxima as they drove off.

"Damn, that is one fine ass brown skin sista," one of the guys said. "Yes, Lady Boss surely is," another one of the men said. "Just don't be too slow or fuck up her money or that fine black woman will turn into the black widow before your ass can even blink," another one of the men said. "I've already seen her work. You don't have to worry about me ever coming up short with her," one of the guys said.

Outside the *Westside-Roses Among Thorns Daycare Center...*

Rocko and Knuckles were inside a black Cadillac parked directly across the street. Rocko watched as people went in and out of the building, as he looked through a small pair of binoculars. Underneath each of their shirts was a loaded 9mm pistol and inside each of their hands was a black ski-mask.

Rocko looked at his watch. The time was now 3:48 p.m. "Twelve more minutes, Knuckles, then it's time to end this bitch," Rocko said, with a devilish grin on his face.

Inside of Heaven's and Coffe's Place...

Heaven and Coffe had just finished counting the seven stacks of money. After they had counted it all, Heaven passed Coffe two of her stacks. Coffe smilingly accepted it. It was the most money she had ever had at once and the fastest ten grand that Coffe had ever made. Heaven picked up her remaining five stacks and put them inside her top dresser drawer.

"What did I tell you, Coffee. If Tony, Jr. wanted the info bad enough he would pay for it," Heaven said. "Do you think he's a little upset that you were playing with him," Coffe said, sitting on the edge of the bed. "Fuck Tony, Jr.! That money is payback money for all the times I had to dress up like Rose and fuck his wrinkled dick father," Heaven said. "We all did it once or twice...that dude was pressed for a piece of Rose," Coffe laughed.

"Who do you think Tony, Jr. is gonna hire for that last dancing position," Coffe said, changing the subject. "I don't know who he will give the job to. I think the pervert just likes seeing naked bitches strip for him. His nasty ass father wanted to fuck everything moving and the apple don't fall to far from the tree. Tony, Jr.'s freak ass gets his kicks out of watching new women strip for him. He might not ever give nobody the job. Then he'll have a different female applying for the position every day. Fucking freak," Heaven said, as Coffe started to crack up laughing.

Westside-Roses Among Thorns Daycare Center...

Inside the large children's play room, Rose stood around her staff of teachers, watching as all the children played. The sounds of boisterous children playing and teachers standing around drinking coffee and gossiping were in full motion .Over a hundred young boys and girls ran around the room enjoying themselves with balls, ropes and toys. However, instead of playing with the other children, Billy was standing next to Rose holding her hand.

As the two masked men entered the playroom, Billy was the first person to see them. The sounds of gunfire filled the room, accompanied by loud piercing screams of panic and fear. People were running all around the room. The place was in total chaos and the two masked men kept firing their weapons in Rose's direction.

147

When Billy saw Rose fall onto a wall and began to slide down onto the floor, he ran over and covered her bleeding body with his. The man fired two more shots at Rose but he missed his target and hit Billy instead. Both bullets hit Billy in his back and his small body slumped down on Rose's chest. Suddenly the two masked men took off and ran out of the door. The screams were coming from all directions and the voice of a woman yelled out, "CALL THE COPS, SOMEBODY PLEASE CALL THE COPS, OH MY GOD!!!"

"Rose is shot!!! And Billy is shot too," someone else yelled out. "So is Mrs. Nelson and little Sally," a child shouted as she began to shake and scream. "And so is Mr. Tucker," an employee yelled, as she made her way to gather the young children who were froze in a panic.

When the police and ambulances finally arrived, the five injured people were all quickly transported to the nearest hospital. No one had known the reason why the two masked men came in and started shooting people. Frantic parents rushed to the daycare and searched for their children. Police officers had to close off the area and they were trying to see if they had any witnesses. The news reporters were already lined up outside of the building searching for answers to their many questions; and gearing up to go live. This shooting would surely be the topic of the day.

Chapter Forty-Nine
A ROSE AMONG THORNS II

Downtown Philadelphia...

Eric and his lawyer, Steve, were inside his office going over some important paperwork. A hard knock at the door startled them.

"Kim, what is it," Steve said, upset that she had disturbed him. The door quickly opened and his secretary stuck her head inside the room. "This better be an emergency," Steve said. "I believe it is, Mr. Steinberg," Kim said, with a scared look in her eyes. "Well, what is it then? Can't you see we're busy here," he shouted.

"The daycare center in West Philly that Mr. Spencer owns has been shot up! It's all over the news," Kim said. "What!!!" Eric said, jumping up from his chair. "What did you say, Kim," Eric repeated, grabbing his briefcase and throwing his papers inside.

"Mr. Spencer, your daycare was shot up and I'm almost positive that ... that ..." she paused, unsure of how to say what she must. "THAT WHAT," Eric yelled. "That your fiancé, Rose, was one of the people who has been shot," she said, as she immediately felt sick to her stomach.

Without saying another word, Eric rushed out of the office.

An Hour Later
Inside the Platinum Club...

"Great fucking job! Great fucking job," Tony, Jr. said, giving Rocko and Knuckles both a hug. "The shit is all over the news," he said, excitedly. "Are y'all sure she's dead? The news reports said that three people died but they didn't give out any of the victims' names," he asked.

"Boss, I'm sure I shot her at least once in the head. But she was running around the room like a scared rabbit inside a cage with a cobra," Rocko laughed. "I shot at her too but there were so many people running around screaming that I'm not sure if I hit her or one of those little bastards that was running around," Knuckles said. "I do remember this kid jumping in front of her. Big mistake," Knuckles continued.

"I'll keep checking the news. Sooner or later we'll find out who survived and who will be visiting my father. One thing for sure is, if Rose ain't one of the dead I won't stop until she is," Tony, Jr. said as he laughed; feeling very pleased with himself.

"I'll see y'all later. Send Butta in," Tony, Jr. said as the men left his office. When Rocko and Knuckles walked out, a petite, beautiful brown-skinned female walked inside the office and shut the door behind her. Tony, Jr. smiled and turned up the music on his CD player. Then he sat down in his chair and said, "Okay, Butta, show me what you got."

Chapter Fifty
A ROSE AMONG THORNS II

"Hello, Edna, what's up," Braheem said, answering his cell phone while driving his truck down Broad Street. "Braheem, meet me at the hospital. It's an emergency," Edna said. "What's wrong with Levi," he asked. "No, meet me at Presbyterian Hospital. I'll be out front with Josh," Edna said. "Edna, why? You know I hate hospitals. What's wrong," Braheem said. "Yo, just meet me," she said. "Just tell me what's going on," Braheem demanded.

"Braheem, Rose just got shot! Something happened at Eric's daycare," Edna finally said. "What the FUCK…" Braheem was lost for words. "Please, just get down here. Eric, Joyce and Rose's family are already here. Hurry up man," Edna said, ending the call.

Braheem made a quick u-turn and headed towards the Presbyterian Hospital in West Philadelphia. He felt tears softly falling onto his cheeks and his stomach ached deeply. Why did Rose have to get shot? What was going on? He was lost and his thoughts had him all over the place.

When he finally arrived at the hospital, Edna and Josh were outside waiting for him. Braheem parked his truck and quickly jumped out.

"Is she alright? What happened? Where's Eric," he said in a panic and without taking a pause.

"Everybody is inside. We been out here waiting on you. You have to go in and find out what's going on, come on," Edna said.

Braheem looked up at the tall hospital building and shook his head. His legs felt heavy but he knew he had to find out if Rose had made it or not. As he rushed through the emergency room sliding doors the fear of the unknown filled him.

Inside of Heaven's and Coffe's Place...

While Heaven was inside of her bedroom counting her money for the third time, Coffe was inside her bedroom lying across the bed watching the six o'clock news. As the news reported the story about the daycare shooting, Coffe's heart filled with sorrow and tears fell from her eyes. Hearing the news reporter talk about the tragic shooting slowly began to eat away at her conscience.

When Rose worked at the Platinum Club, they were good friends. Rose had never showed her anything but love and kindness. Now Coffe lay across her bed feeling like a piece of shit. She had crossed Rose and for what, some money.

As the tears continued to fall down Coffe's face, she reached for the remote control and turned off the TV. She needed to take her mind off the situation and focus on something else. That something else was her lover Edna. She knew once they got together later on that night, Edna's sensual touch and comfort would ease her mind.

Heaven, unaware of the happenings of the day, put the stacks of money back into her top dresser drawer and closed it. Braheem had called her earlier in the day and told her that he would be over later that night. Just the thought of her young, handsome lover fucking her all night long had her wet with anticipation.

Heaven walked over to her bedroom door and locked it, and then she walked back over to her bed and sat down. She reached under the mattress and took out a small vibrator. After Heaven took off her bra and panties, she laid her naked body on the bed.

As she turned on the vibrator she closed her eyes. Slowly she started rubbing it across her breasts and then she guided her hand down to her wetness. The feeling was wonderful and therapeutic. In less than five minutes, Heaven had giving herself an orgasm. After relaxing her body for a few minutes, Heaven got up and made her way to the shower.

The warm water caressed her body and all she could think about was her handsome ghetto knight, and how in just a few hours he would finish the job she had started.

Chapter Fifty-One
A ROSE AMONG THORNS II

Inside the crowded hospital emergency room, family and friends of all the shooting victims sat around talking, crying and praying to hear some good news from the doctors. Eric sat over in a corner alone. His head was down to the floor. The doctors hadn't said a word about any of the victims yet and the long wait was taking its toll on Eric.

Braheem stood by the large glass door, looking out at Edna and Josh who were outside talking to each other. The soft tap on his shoulder startled him. He turned around quickly and saw that it was Joyce, whose eyes were filled with tears.

"Braheem, we need to talk. I have something very important to tell you," she said. "Joyce, please!!! Not right now. Can't you see that I have a lot on my mind? Rose is shot so right now nothing is more important than that," Braheem fumed, as he walked out of the door.

Later That Night
Southwest Philly...

For two long hours, Willie and Sanchez had been driving around looking for trouble. The streets of Southwest Philly were dark and pretty much empty. The only people that appeared to be outside on this chilly fall night were cops and crack heads.

Willie pulled his car up at a red light and stopped. He was a few blocks down from Bartram High School. The same high school he had dropped out of in the tenth grade. Sanchez sat inside the passenger seat, holding a loaded .45 Smith and Wesson. The AK-47 was lying on the back seat, loaded and ready to do some major damage. Before the red light had changed, Willie noticed three crack heads walking down the street; two were men and there was one woman.

"Oh, shit! That's Ms. Gayle," Willie said, looking out the window. "Who," Sanchez said curiously. "Ms. Gayle is Josh's mother! The bitch used to be fine when I was younger but now she's nothing more than a strung out crack head," Willie said, quickly pulling his car over and beeping the horn.

"Ms. Gayle! Ms. Gayle! How you doing," Willie said, rolling down his tinted window. Gayle could not see who it was inside the truck, so she walked up closer to investigate. Her two male friends stood back and waited for her. Willie quickly got out the car. Gayle was too high to recognize who the stranger was.

"Josh told me to come find you! He's in some serious trouble," Willie lied. "What? What's wrong with my baby," Gayle shouted. "He's at the hospital. Get in the back and I'll take you to go see him," Willie said. Sanchez had already moved the AK-47.

"Slim, Pete, I'll see y'all tomorrow. Something is wrong with my baby," Gayle said, before opening the back door and getting inside. Willie quickly got back inside the truck and sped off down the street.

155

While Gayle sat in the back seat crying, Willie and Sanchez had evil smirks on their faces. Twenty minutes later the truck pulled up to a dark wooded area inside Fairmount Park.

"This ain't the hospital," Gayle said in a scared voice. "No, it ain't," Willie said getting out the truck. Gayle never saw the sucka punch coming but the force from Sanchez's blow knocked her out cold. Willie and Sanchez dragged Gayle from out of the truck. Her thin body lay still on the ground. Willie quickly pulled out his loaded 9mm and aimed it at her head.

"Hold up, Willie! Hold up! Let me fuck this bitch first," Sanchez said excitedly. "Do you but we ain't got all night," Willie said. Sanchez quickly pulled down Gayle's pants and panties. Then he slid down his jeans and climbed on top of Gayle's motionless body and started fucking her while she was still unconscious.

When Gayle started coming back around, Sanchez was still on top of her. After he had finally climaxed, he stood up and pulled his jeans up.

"Go get the black marker," Willie told Sanchez. Willie looked into Gayle's dazed and confused eyes. When Sanchez came back, he had the marker and they both pointed their guns at Gayle.

"Blame this one on your son," Willie said, as they squeezed their triggers and sent countess slugs into her body.

Chapter Fifty-Two
A ROSE AMONG THORNS II

Presbyterian Hospital...

Inside Rose's hospital room, Eric sat by her bed holding her hand. The bullet that had entered her upper right shoulder had just missed her head by inches. Rose had only suffered minimal damage but unfortunately all the victims had not been so lucky.

Eric was in tears and he had never been more afraid in all his life. Just the thought of losing Rose was worse than death itself. Eric was so lost and very confused. Whoever was behind hurting his Rose would suffer and this was a promise he had made to himself.

When Rose opened her eyes the first person she saw was Eric. She reached out her left hand and wiped away his tears.

"Where did everybody go," Rose said weakly. "After you went back to sleep they all went home. Joyce and our mothers said they'll be back up here tomorrow, as soon as visiting hours start up again," Eric said softly. "Where's Braheem," Rose said. "He came but left out. He said he couldn't take seeing you like this," Eric said. "Did he and Joyce talk? She has something to tell him," Rose said very dimly.

"They talked for a few minutes but then he left out. He wasn't here too long. You know Braheem don't like hospitals," Eric said.
"Why didn't you go home and rest? The doctors said I'll be fine. You could just come back in the morning,

"Rose suggested. "I'm not going nowhere. We gonna walk out this place together," Eric said seriously.

A big smile came to Rose's face. "Now you see how I felt when you got shot, Rose said, as she continued to smile. "How is everyone else doing that got hurt? Did you find out or did I fall asleep on you," Rose said. Eric looked into Rose's eyes and sadly shook his head.

"Mrs. Nelson, Sally and Billy all died," Eric said. "Billy! No, Eric, not Billy! Please, Eric! Please don't tell me Billy is gone," Rose cried. Eric stood up and held Rose in his arms.

"Baby, I'm sorry! I'm truly sorry but Billy is gone," he said. As the flow of tears fell down from their faces, they remained embraced in each other's arms.

"He saved my life," Rose said into Eric's ear. "He jumped in front of the bullets to save me," she wept. "I know. One of the teachers told me," Eric said. "Why, Eric? Why? Tell me why, Eric," Rose cried out. "I don't know why Baby, but I promise you I'll find out," Eric assured her.

"Eric, please don't get into trouble…too much has happened already. Promise me you won't do nothing stupid! You've come too far. Don't let the streets pull you back," Rose said, staring into Eric's watery eyes. "Baby, I'm sorry, but I can't promise you nothing but my love," Eric whispered softly.

As the medication took a hold of Rose's weak and tired body, Eric went into the visitor's room and began placing calls. He was determined to find out who was behind the shooting and to get his revenge.

Chapter Fifty-Three
A ROSE AMONG THORNS II

Early Tuesday Morning...

When Edna opened up her eyes, Coffe was sitting on the edge of the bed in tears. Edna quickly jumped up and sat by her side. She looked deeply into Coffe's watery brown eyes. Edna noticed Coffe had been on edge all night long but didn't know why. Now, after seeing the sad expression on Coffe's face, Edna knew that something was up.

"What's wrong, Coffe? You've been moody all night. Tell me what's bothering you," Edna said, wrapping her arm around Coffe's shoulder. Coffe stared into Edna's serious eyes and said, "You know that daycare that got shot up yesterday..."
"Yeah, what about it," Edna said anxiously.
"I know who did it and I know why they did it," Coffe said.

Edna had a shocked expression on her face. She couldn't believe what Coffe had just said.

"You know who did it," Edna stood up and said. "Yeah, I know everything! I even got paid for helping my girlfriend, Heaven, get the info Tony, Jr. wanted," Coffe cried out. "Hold up a bit and slow down. I need you to start from the very beginning," Edna said.

Edna sat back down beside Coffe and looked into her tearful eyes. After she reached out and grabbed Coffe's hand, she said, "Now baby, tell me everything and don't leave out a single word."

For the next half hour, Coffe told Edna everything that she had known. She told Edna about Tony, Jr. and his obsession with watching women dance for him, about Rose, Rocko and Knuckles, Heaven's greed, the money, the club, and anything else she thought was relevant. When Coffe finally finished she felt relieved to get it all out of her system. Edna sat there in total disbelief. She couldn't believe what she had just heard.

After Edna and Coffe had taken a shower together they quickly got dressed. The first person that Edna called was Eric and then Braheem, but he didn't answer his cell phone. Edna asked Coffe to call her place and to see if Braheem or Heaven was there but she got no answer. Edna called Braheem again but he was still not available, so she made a fast call to Josh.

Within thirty minutes Eric and Josh were headed to Edna's apartment but Braheem still was nowhere to be found.

Inside Heaven's Bedroom...

Braheem had Heaven's hands handcuffed to the headboard. Her long, sexy legs were resting on top of his broad shoulders as his hard dick slid in and out of her wet pussy.

"Ummm... Yes!!!" Heaven moaned out. "It's your pussy, Daddy! Fuck this wet pussy like you own it," Heaven yelled out.

Braheem had Heaven's legs gripped up as he gave her long, powerful strokes. "Yes, Braheem!! Fuck me! Tear this pussy up with that big ass dick!!!

This is your pussy," Heaven screamed. When Heaven talked dirty to Braheem it only turned him on more, and after he had cum twice his dick was still hard.

'Fuck me, Braheem," Heaven yelled out, as her third orgasm swept through her trembling body. "I'm cuming, I'm ... cuming!!!" Heaven cried out in ecstasy.

Their naked bodies were covered in sweat and Braheem continued stroking her juicy kitty-cat. A lot was on his mind but Braheem was determined to fuck away his problems.

Heaven laid back, still handcuffed to the bed, as she received the best sex her body had ever known. Her moans, grunts and screams were so loud that the people next door could hear her. She continued to scream out her lover's name as his thick dick entered her flood gates.

"Braheem, I...love...you!! I love this dick," she screamed out. After Braheem had come for the third time his tired body fell down on top of Heaven's. They both lay in bed breathing hard and heavy as their bodies recuperated from their intense sexual feast. Braheem's cell phone and Heaven's house phone were both ringing at the same time, and his pager was vibrating on the floor. Now that they were quiet they could finally hear the calls coming in. However, both were too exhausted to answer.

Braheem got up a bit of energy. He grabbed the handcuff key from off the nightstand, and he unlocked Heaven's hands from the headboard. For a few more moments they lay in bed trying to calm their bodies and focus their energy on the phone calls coming in.

Finally, Braheem reached out and grabbed his cell phone. When he saw Eric's name on the caller ID screen he quickly answered.

"Eric, what's up…" he said, as he listened in. "What? Yeah! I'm on my way now," Braheem said, getting his tired body out of bed.

"Baby, where you running off to," Heaven said softly. "I got an emergency," Braheem said, rushing into the bathroom.

When he came out of the bathroom, Heaven was snoring lightly under the sheets. After Braheem got dressed, he quickly left out the apartment and headed towards Edna's. Once again his mind was clouded with thoughts and his heart filled with fear of the unknown.

Chapter Fifty-Four
A ROSE AMONG THORNS II

Rose had just finished eating breakfast when her doctor came in to check up on her injured shoulder. He shared a brief chat with her and left back out of the room. Rose was a bit bored because in the absence of her family or friends she didn't have much to do. She didn't want to watch TV or listen to the radio, because any talk of the shootings at the daycare deeply depressed and scared her.

All night long she had thoughts about little Billy and she was unable to sleep. The only two people who survived their wounds were Rose and the math teacher, Mr. Tucker. He was in critical but stable condition. A bullet had pierced his kidney but he was still hanging on.

Rose talked to Joyce for a bit, but after the two hung up she needed something else to do. She pressed her call button and politely asked her nurse for a pencil and pad. The nurse quickly brought in both items and asked if she needed anything further, but Rose was happy with the pen and pad for the moment.

As the flow of tears fell down from Rose's eyes, she did what she always did to help heal her pain and confusion. Rose started writing.

Heaven is Just a Breath Away

I know you're looking down on us all crying from all of our wrongs
The greatest gift is life but we don't appreciate it until it's finally gone
I know you're only a breath away
I can feel it when I look high above
I know you cry when men kill for money and when women beg for their love
Heaven, you take us without warning
sometimes even before we are formed
The elderly you take after many years on earth
while some infants you take as soon as they're born
I know you're just a breath away
adding more and more on your chosen list
Snatching up all of those perfect souls until this ugly world no longer exists
The killing, adultery, and betrayal, the envy, hate and all the lies will never enter your paradise
Into that world beyond your heavenly skies
Most people think you're only a myth
so many don't believe you're actually real
So they ignore all of your warnings until their fate is quickly revealed
But I know you're alive and well
That's why I'll always truly believe
That heaven is just a breath away
So when it's my time, I'll be ready to leave.

Rose

Chapter Fifty-Five
A ROSE AMONG THORNS II

"Are you fuckin serious," Braheem said, after hearing everything that Coffe had just told him. Braheem shook his head in disbelief. How could this happen right up under his nose. "That's why y'all kept mentioning the daycares," he said angrily.

Edna and Josh sat beside each other on the sofa while Eric stood by the front window in deep thought.

"So Tony, Jr. is Perotta's son, huh," Braheem said to himself. "I'm gonna kill that muthafucka," Braheem yelled. "Calm down, Braheem. Everything will be alright," Eric said calmly. "But Eric, he's behind the shooting at the daycare! Three people are dead, one in critical condition and Rose almost lost her life!!! Plus, Coffe said that Tony, Jr. won't rest until Rose is dead though. How can you tell me to calm down and why are you so damn calm," Braheem asked.

"Because I just thought of an idea that will take care of this whole mess and Coffe I'm gonna need your help," Eric said.

When Eric walked over to the sofa everybody gathered around and listened to what he had to say. After Eric finished telling them what he wanted everyone to do, Coffe made a call to Tony, Jr. Once she hung up the phone she had a big smile plastered on her face.

"Everything is set. He bit," Coffe said.

"Okay, everyone knows what to do now. Make this fast and flawless. Braheem, I want you to call me when everything is finished," Eric said, shaking everyone's hand.

"Where are you going," Braheem asked. "Back to the hospital to be there for my wife," Eric said. He looked at Edna and winked. Edna winked back because she had always admired Eric. He was there for his family and a very smart man. Edna always had a secret crush on Eric but she kept those feelings to herself. Eric was the one who gave her the nickname "Lady Boss" and it made her like it that much more. Edna was loyal to Eric and Braheem, and she had no problem putting her life on the line for either one of them.

"Good luck. I'll see y'all later," Eric said, as he walked out of the apartment and closed the door behind him.

Forty Minutes Later...

Braheem pulled his Navigator in front of Heaven's condominium and parked. Edna and Josh pulled up beside him and parked as well. Coffe remained inside the car with Edna and the two ladies were going over what they needed to do. Josh kept watch. Inside Edna's secret compartment in the car she had her 9mm with the attached silencer, and today seemed like a good day to put it to use, she thought.

Braheem got out of his truck and used Coffe's key to enter the apartment. When he walked inside the place was very quiet. He walked back into

Heaven's bedroom. She was still sleeping. Tired from all the fucking she and Braheem had done. Braheem pulled out his .40 caliber and stood over Heaven's sleeping body. He thought about the hour earlier when he was fucking her brains out, but that was the past.

"Wake up, bitch," Braheem yelled, as he smacked Heaven upside the head with his right hand. Heaven quickly jumped up on the bed. When she saw Braheem standing over her and holding a gun in her face she couldn't believe it.

"Braheem, what's wrong? Baby, what is it," she cried out. "Bitch, don't call me your baby! You're nothing but a money hungry whore!!! Bitch, I know about everything! About your jealousy for Rose, the daycare, Tony, Jr. and the money you got to set Rose up," Braheem yelled out. "Baby, please! I love you! Please don't do this to us! Please, I'm sorry," Heaven cried out.

"Rose is family. That's my cousin's fiancé you greedy ass bitch! Three people are dead because of your greedy ass and two of them are children! I bet you don't even care! Pretty bitches like you only give a fuck about yourselves," Braheem said, reaching out and grabbing Heaven's throat.

Instantly her face started to sweat. He saw the look of fear in her eyes and he enjoyed it. Heaven saw the look of a born killer in his and she was petrified.

"Bitch, I should kill you right now," Braheem said, ignoring her tears and cries. "Bitches like you, Heaven, fuck things up for all the good bitches out there. Our time is now over, Bitch," he said, finally releasing his strong grip from her neck.

Heaven fell back on the bed and she grasped for air. Her neck was very tender and she was scared to death. What was he going to do next? She had fucked up and that was all she could think about.

Braheem walked over to the top dresser drawer and opened it. He took out the five stacks of money and threw them at her.

"Is twenty-five thousand dollars worth three lives," he shouted out angrily. "Braheem, please! Please don't leave me! I love you! I swear I love you," Heaven begged. "Bitch, you don't even know what love is! Your lover is money and that same lover has become your downfall. You haven't once said you were sorry or said anything about the trauma you've caused. You keep askin about me when that is a dead issue," he said in all seriousness.

"Braheem, I am sorry. I really am. Just let me make it up to you! You can have all the money. I just want you! Please don't do this to us! Please, baby, I ... love ... you," Heaven cried.

Braheem walked back over to the bed and looked into Heaven's terrified eyes.

"Bitch, don't ever call me again! And I mean it! Or the next time I see you I won't be so nice," Braheem said, turning around and walking away.

"Please, Braheem! Please come back! Please don't leave me like this," Heaven cried out. Braheem walked out of the front door as Heaven's cries fell onto deaf ears.

Later That Afternoon...

When Eric walked into Rose's hospital room, Joyce was sitting in a chair next to the bed. Eric had a large white teddy bear in his arms. He walked over to Rose and sat the teddy bear beside her.

"I'll be right back, don't move," he said, jokingly walking back out of the room. A few moments later Eric returned into the room with a handful of *Get Well Soon* balloons and a card. Rose and Joyce smiled at each other upon seeing the gifts.

After tying the balloons to her bed, Eric walked over to Rose and gave her an elongated loving kiss. Joyce enjoyed seeing her friends happy and their affection only made her miss Braheem more. Eric pulled up an empty chair and sat down beside Joyce. He gave his Lil Sis a loving hug.

"Did you think about our talk," Eric asked her. "Yes, Eric, and don't worry I won't mess up no more...once he comes back," Joyce said. "You just missed my mom and my brothers," Rose said. "No I didn't. I caught them leaving out when I came in," Eric said. "Did you talk to my father," Rose asked curiously. "Yeah, Johnny Ray called me about a half hour ago. I told him everything that happened and of course he was a little shaken up, but I assured him that everything was okay. He's feeling better now and he loves you. We talked about his lawyer and some other stuff," Eric continued.

"What did the lawyer say," Rose said excitingly. "Johnny Ray told me that things are looking good for now and for everybody to keep praying," Eric said, reaching out and grabbing Rose's hand.

"Where's Braheem," Rose asked. "He's taking care of something for me... maybe he'll be here later. You know how much he dislikes hospitals," Eric said.

Joyce stood up from her chair and she gave Rose and Eric each a kiss and a hug.

"I'll let you two lovebirds be alone. I have to pick up Ryan from my mother's house anyway. Then I have to go home and do some more writing," Joyce smiled. "Writing," Eric said confused because he had never heard or saw Joyce take an interest in writing.

"Yeah, writing! I've been doing a lot of writing lately and it seems to help. Ain't that right, Rose," Joyce said. "That's right," Rose winked. Eric and Rose watched Joyce walk out of the room. When she was gone Eric sat his chair closer to Rose.

"Baby, the balloons, the card and the teddy bear are so beautiful," Rose said. "Not as beautiful as you are," Eric grinned. "I closed the Westside center down for a few weeks. At least until things are calmed down. A lot of the parents are afraid for their children's lives, which I can understand. Once you're able we're gonna have a community meeting with everybody. The teachers, parents, children, and the neighbors to assure them that what happened will never happen again. I have already talked to a security firm that will install high-tech security systems, and I'm going to have armed guards in all the centers from now on," Eric said.

"Thank you, Eric," Rose said, as the thought of the incident brought tears to her eyes. "I also had a talk with the people who had family members pass on. I'm going to pay for their funerals," Eric said sadly. "Baby, I love you so much," Rose said, reaching out and giving Eric a long hug. She was so grateful that he took it upon himself to help the victims' families out. That was the least they could offer.

Chapter Fifty-Six
A ROSE AMONG THORNS II

Outside The Platinum Club...

Braheem and Josh sat inside his Navigator truck watching as Coffe and Edna walked into the club. They sat there patiently waiting with their guns underneath their shirts. Eric had devised a brilliant plan and now all everyone had to do was execute their part. Coffe and Edna walked upstairs and were greeted by Rocko and Knuckles, who stood out front of Tony, Jr.'s office.

"I have a new dancer for Tony, Jr. to audition. We were supposed to meet him at 2:30," Coffe said, as she gave the men a seductive smile. "One second, Coffe, wait right here," Rocko said, knocking on the door. "Come in," Tony, Jr. shouted out.

Rocko walked inside the office and closed the door behind him.

"What is it," Tony, Jr. said, sitting at his desk reading the newspaper and the story about the daycare massacre. "Boss, Coffe is out front with another dancer. She said you were expecting her at 2:30," Rocko said. "Yeah, I was. What do she look like," Tony, Jr. asked, laying down the paper and standing up from his chair.

"She's a beauty, just the way you like 'em," Rocko smiled. "Oh, really? Well send her in," Tony, Jr. said, walking around his desk and sitting down on the edge of it.

When Edna walked into Tony Jr.'s office, his eyes popped open with lust.

"How are you doing today, sir," Edna said, closing the door behind her. "Call me Tony, Jr.," he said smilingly. Edna had on a tight-fitted black dress that showed off her cleavage and accentuated her deep honey brown frame. Her black hair was cut in a short stylish Halle Berry style. Her eyebrows were perfectly arched and a clear shiny lip gloss covered her sexy full lips. The Chanel perfume she had on instantly filled the room, and Tony, Jr. was very pleased with the beautiful black woman who stood in front of him. Of all the women who had auditioned for him, Edna, by far, was the most attractive; with an amazing body as well.

Tony, Jr. walked over to the music player and put on a song.

"Do you have something slow and mellow," Edna asked. "Sure, I got Mary J, Sade, Brandy, Monica, whoever you want to hear," Tony, Jr. said, going through his collection of CDs. "Do you have R. Kelly's *Your Body's Calling,*" Edna said, flirtatiously. "Sure do," Tony, Jr. said, grabbing the classic 12-play CD and putting it in the sound system.

Before the song came on, Tony, Jr. sat back down on his desk and said, "So, pretty, you never told me your name." Edna looked into his lustful eyes and said, "They call me Lady Boss." Tony, Jr. crossed his arms and smiled. "Now this is one woman that I would fuck," he said so softly that Edna couldn't hear him.

When the music started playing from out of the speakers, Edna began a slow, sensual dance.

173

Tony, Jr. lustfully watched as Edna moved her sexy body to the smooth rhythm of the song. His dick was now growing inside his pants. Edna stood in front of Tony, Jr. gracefully moving her body and licking her juicy full lips. Her erotic dance had Tony, Jr. hard as a rock. Slowly, Edna began sliding down her dress, and as the song played she never lost a step.

Edna slid the tight fitted dress down past her chest, letting Tony, Jr. see her beautiful brown, voluptuous breasts. His breathing became heavy. Edna looked into his lustful eyes and smiled. She could always recognize a sucker when she saw one and now this sucker was front and center.

As Edna continued her dance, Tony, Jr. was so caught up into her erotic performance that he never paid attention to the black belt strapped around her waist. Quickly, Edna reached behind her back and grabbed the loaded 9mm that had a silencer attached. When she brought her hand back around, the gun was now pointed at Tony, Jr.'s head. Before he could run or yell for help, Edna fired two silent, but deadly shots into Tony, Jr.'s head. One entered right between his lustful eyes. Tony, Jr.'s large body fell onto his desk before sliding onto the floor. And just like his father, Perotta, he died filled with lust and with a hard dick.

Edna quickly ran over and turned Tony, Jr.'s body onto his stomach. Since the music was loud and still playing, no one outside the door had heard a thing. Besides, Coffe was outside the door keeping the two bodyguards distracted, just like Eric had told her to do. Edna put her dress back on and hid the gun behind her back. When she opened up the door, she screamed, "Hurry up! Something is wrong with Tony, Jr.....he fainted!"

Rocko and Knuckles quickly left Coffe and ran into the office. When they saw Tony, Jr.'s body lying on the ground, they ran over beside him. The first thing they noticed was a small pool of blood that surrounded his head. When they turned around to see where Edna was, she was waiting with a big grin on her face.

"Suckas," Edna said, aiming her 9mm at them and shooting both men in their heads and chests. She emptied the entire clip, and she then watched as both bodies fell down beside their dead boss.

Coffe walked over to the desk and opened the top drawer. She knew all about the secret safe Tony, Jr. had hidden inside of his office. All the dancers had heard about it but they didn't know exactly where it was. Coffe and Edna looked all around the office. Then Coffe noticed the large portrait of Mr. Perotta and walked over to it. She removed the picture from the wall and "Bingo," Coffe said, because she had discovered the hiding spot.

To both of their surprise the safe was unlocked. Coffe and Edna looked into the safe and saw all the stacks of money sitting inside.

"Go get Josh and tell him to bring me the two green duffle bags. Tell Braheem to stay in the car and keep a watch out on things," Edna said to Coffe, as she kept her eyes on the money in the safe.

Coffe rushed out of the office and ran to get Josh and tell Braheem what Edna said. Moments later, Josh and Coffe returned to the office. Josh quickly ran over to Edna and together they started filling up the duffle bags with the money. Coffe wiped everything they had touched down with a rag she had inside her purse. Braheem sat inside his truck scoping out the scene and making sure that there were no surprises. He had a lot of memories of the Platinum Club; some good and others not so good.

Braheem took out his cell phone and called Eric on his phone. Eric quickly answered. "Yo, talk to me. I'm here with my baby so make it fast," he said. "You were right, like father, like son," Braheem said. "I'll talk to you later," Braheem said, closing his cell phone.

After Edna and Josh had put all the money into the duffle bags, they carried them over to the door.

"Coffe, you know what to do. Hurry up and meet us back outside," Edna said, as she and Josh carried the heavy duffle bag out the office and down the hall and stairs. Coffe opened up her purse and took out two Cuban cigars. She lit them both and then sat one on top of Tony, Jr.'s leather chair. Then she placed another on the carpeted floor. Seeing the smoke ascend into the air, Coffe grabbed the rag and used it to wipe off the desk drawer. She also wiped off the safe and both doorknobs before she left out the room and shut it tightly behind her.

When Coffe walked out of the door, Edna was sitting inside her car waiting for her; and the duffle bags were lying on the back seat. Josh was inside of Braheem's truck.

Thirty minutes after they had left the Platinum Club, the building was engulfed in flames and the three bodies inside were all burned beyond recognition. Dental records would have to be used to identify their corpses.

After they had gotten back to Edna's apartment, they began counting the money and talking about what had happened. It took them almost five hours to finish counting it all; and without the help of the currency counter they might have been there for days. When they were done the sum was one million, two hundred and fifty thousand dollars; which was neatly laid out all across the living room table and floor.

Edna passed Coffe fifty thousand dollars for the part she played, and then she sent her into the bedroom to wait for her. Coffe eagerly grabbed her money and walked away with a big smile on her face. Braheem grabbed one of the duffle bags and put five hundred thousand inside of it.

"That's Eric's," he said. Edna and Josh both agreed. Especially since Eric was the mastermind of the scheme. Braheem, Edna and Josh equally split up the rest of the money before the two fellas departed.

When Edna entered the bedroom, Coffe's naked body was laying on top of a bed full of cash. "Now my body's calling for you," Coffe said in a seductive tone. Edna was surely ready to answer that call.

Chapter Fifty-Seven
A ROSE AMONG THORNS II

Lewisburg Federal Prison...

The CO walked over to Johnny Ray's cell and tapped on the thick steel bar. Johnny Ray was lost in thought. The news about the daycare shootings had him feeling very uneasy and confused.

"Johnny Ray, you got a visit," the tall white CO said. "A visit? From who? It's Tuesday," Johnny Ray said, with a bemused expression on his face. "It's your attorney. I guess he called the warden and requested a prisoner-attorney visit. Get dressed. I'll be back in ten minutes," the CO said, walking down the tier.

Johnny Ray quickly jumped off his bunk and started putting on his pants. His celly was on the top bunk silently reading the Quran.

"What do you think, Abdul," Johnny Ray said, putting his shirt on. "Maybe it's something good. Any time a lawyer comes to visit a prisoner at the prison, it's usually for a very good reason," Abdul said, closing his Quran and sitting up on his bunk.

After Johnny Ray had gotten dressed, Abdul looked at him and said, "Ain't you forgetting something my brother," Johnny Ray looked up at Abdul and smiled. "Yeah, you're right," Johnny Ray said, getting down on his knees and saying a quick silent prayer. Even though Johnny Ray was Christian and Abdul was a Sunni Muslim, they were good friends. Since the first day Johnny Ray was brought into Lewisburg Federal Prison, he and Abdul had hit it off. Both men had a great deal of respect for the other, despite their different religious beliefs.

When the CO returned back to the cell, he opened the cell, and then handcuffed Johnny Ray's hands behind his back. Abdul got up from off his bunk and walked over to the front of the cell, as he watched the CO escort his celly down the tier.

"Allah, please help that good brother make it back home to his family," he said.

Inside of Heaven's Condominium...

Heaven sat at the edge of her bed, letting the stream of tears fall down her face. She hadn't realize just how caught up she was with Braheem, until he cursed her out and walked out of the front door. In the short time the two had shared, Heaven had let her guard down and allowed herself to have feelings for him. This was something she just didn't do. Sex with Braheem was the best she had ever had and the thought of never feeling his body beside hers again was hard to accept. For the first time in her life, Heaven was sexually whipped. This young stud had come into her life and now he was gone.

As she stared at the money on the bed she wished she could turn back the hands of time. Inside her quiet bedroom Heaven sat on her bed in a state of shock. No words could express the feelings racing through her body.

When she turned on the news and saw the story about the Platinum Club burning down her heart sank even lower. As the tears continued to fall down her face, Heaven could only shake her head in disbelief. Today had been the worst day of her entire life. There was nothing left for her in Philly and she knew that soon it would be time for her to relocate.

Later That Night...

When Braheem walked into the house, Joyce was sitting on the sofa listening to Mary J. Blige and writing on a yellow notepad. Her female intuition had told her that he would come home tonight. That's why she had scented candles burning all around the house and Ryan was already sleeping in his comfortable bed.

Braheem shut the door and took off his jacket. He walked over to Joyce and sat down beside her. For a moment they each stared into each other's eyes. They missed each other and they didn't need words to express that. Braheem reached out and grabbed Joyce's hands.

"Baby, I'm sorry for...," he started but was interrupted. "No, I'm sorry for running you away," Joyce said. "I'm sorry for being selfish, greedy, spoiled, conceited, lazy and immature," Joyce said, as the tears started falling onto her cheeks. "I'm sorry for not being your rock, your soldier, or your queen and confidant! I'm sorry, Braheem, and baby I promise you that it will never, ever, ever, happen again," Joyce said. "I don't want you to hire no more maid services because from now on Imma clean up my own house, cook us meals every day and play my position the way I should have been. And after I give birth to our newborn child, I'm going to go back to school."

"Newborn child," Braheem said, shocked to hear the news. Joyce looked into Braheem's eyes and said, "Yes, you heard me…newborn child. I'm two months pregnant with our child," she said.

Braheem was speechless. His ears couldn't believe what they had just heard.

"I'm gonna be a father," he said as the tears started falling down his face. "Yes, Braheem, you're gonna be a father," Joyce said, as they began kissing.

Braheem looked into Joyce's eyes and put his hand on her small plumped stomach. "That's my baby in there," he said. "Yes, Braheem, it's your baby. Maybe even the son you've always wanted," Joyce said softly.

For the next hour Braheem and Joyce talked about everything that had happened since the night he walked out of the house. He told Joyce everything about his relationship with Heaven, the Platinum Club, Tony, Jr., the fire-bombing of the house, the money and everything else he could remember. Though the news of her man sleeping with another woman was hard to hear, she wasn't upset with him. He was being honest and she wanted to put the past to rest. They had the rest of their lives to work on their future and that was her priority.

Braheem looked at the yellow notepad that Joyce had been writing on and said, "What's this?" "Oh, it's just a few poems I've been writing. I started writing a few nights ago and it helps me a lot. Braheem flipped through Joyce's notepad. Then he saw a title that caught his attention.

"What's this about," he said. Joyce took the notepad from out of his hand. When she saw the poem he was talking about, she smiled. "Oh, you like that one? I was reading this novel by this guy named Jimmy DaSaint and he wrote a poem in it called *If Prison Takes Me Away*. I liked it so I wrote a response to his poem. Mine is called, *If Prison Takes You Away*," Joyce said.

"Okay, baby, let me hear it," Braheem said, sitting back onto the comfy couch. Joyce grabbed the remote control and turned off the sound system.

"Are you ready," she said. "I'm ready," Braheem said.

You asked me if prison takes you away what will I do
I would ride like the true queen I am and never abandon you
Baby, if prison took you away and I can't handle you being gone
Then every visit I'll be the first in line to let you know you're not in this alone
No, I won't forget about the great sex and all the kinky things you did
No, I won't leave you in the beginning and then try to come back at the end of your bid
I won't start some phony arguments or disrespect you in your face
See once I've accepted you into my heart no other man can take your place
I know that times will be hard for me and many nights I'll be upset and just cry
But I'ma keep it all the way thorough and never betray our love with lies

*I won't chase after the next baller and break our
loving bond
Or try to move forward without you and leave you
hurting behind
I don't care how many years they give you because
together we will do this time
I'ma hold you down till the very last day so when you
return you will still be mine.*

     Braheem sat there speechless. He knew Joyce
had meant every single word she wrote and he was
getting a bit emotional. She was his rock that could
not be broken, and every man needed a strong
woman like her. Braheem grabbed Joyce's hands and
they both stood up from the sofa. Once again they
started kissing, and as their tongues locked in a
sensual dance they started tearing each other's clothes
off.

     Moments later, their two naked bodies were
rolling on top of the carpet. As they made powerful,
passionate love together, nothing but sexual bliss and
ecstasy filled the air. At the top of the stairs, little
Ryan sat smiling. He was happy to see Braheem back
in the house and his mother happy. He went back into
his bedroom and the two lovers made love into the
morning hours.

Chapter Fifty-Eight
A ROSE AMONG THORNS II

Wednesday Morning
Inside Their West Philly Apartment...

Willie and Sanchez sat inside the living room talking. "Man, I need to get out of this apartment and get me some fresh air," Sanchez griped. "Tonight homeboy. Tonight we'll strap up and go out searching for more rivals," Willie laughed. "I'm talking about pussy, Willie! I need you to drop me off at Shanika's house," Sanchez said. "Man, I told you that that bitch is trouble. Women like Shanika know too many niggaz. Too many of our enemies," Willie said sternly.

"Willie, chill man, it's not that serious. I just want some pussy, that's all! Plus, I keep my gun on me at all times. Even when I'm fucking her," Sanchez laughed. "Why do you even mess with that slut," Willie asked. "Because that slut got the best pussy in West Philly and the best blow job on the planet," Sanchez laughed again. "If you want to see that whore then call you a cab cause I ain't taking no chances on getting caught out there slipping," Willie said angrily, walking back into his bedroom. After Willie went into his room and shut the door, Sanchez took out his cell phone and called Shanika.

"Hello, who dis," she answered. "It's me, Sanchez," he said. "Who," she said. "Sanchez," he said louder. "Oh, my bad boo, I couldn't hear you.

My kids playing in the back. About time you called a bitch! When can I taste some of my Papi," Shanika flirted. "Imma call a cab and come over. I'll be there in about an hour or so. Make sure them little bastards you got running around is sleep when I get there too," he said.

"Don't worry, Papi, they'll be in their bedroom with the door closed. I been waiting for you to call me," Shanika said. "Oh, yeah," Sanchez smilingly said. "Yup, I got something special for you when you come through, so make sure you take a Viagra cause you're gonna need one," Shanika said, before hanging up her phone.

After Shanika hung up, Sanchez quickly called the Yellow Cab service and waited for one of their cabs to pick him up. At that same time Shanika sat on her bed in disbelief. She couldn't believe the sudden change of luck that had just come her way. She quickly dialed a number and a female's voice picked up on the first ring.

"Hello, it's me, Shanika. One of your snakes has left his garden and he's on his way over here in a cab," Shanika said. "Lady Boss is that reward still twenty-five thousand dollars," Shanika asked. It sure is and thanks for your services. Make sure you rock him to sleep," Edna said. "Don't worry, I'll fuck him right to sleep," Shanika said, hanging up the telephone.

Shanika sat back on the couch as she anxiously waited for her victim. She looked over at her four young children and thought of how that money would make life a lot better for them. At twenty-one years of age, unmarried, and with four young children, from four different fathers, her bills were way overdue and she had no concerns about what she was about to do. She needed the money and Sanchez would help her get it…even if he would end up with the short end of the stick.

Inside The Philadelphia Coroner's Office…

Josh sat inside the small lobby with Braheem by his side. He had gotten an early morning call from the medical examiner's office, asking him to come downtown to identify the body of his mother. His mother's corpse was found by two young boys who had been walking in Fairmount Park. She had been listed as a Jane Doe for two day until her dental records identified her.

Gayle Ashley Muhamed had been shot multiple times at close range, and with two different guns; a 9mm and a .45 caliber handgun.

When Josh looked at his mother's disfigured corpse, he threw up his breakfast and ran out of the room. Written on his mother's back, in black marker, were the words: *NEVER SLEEP ON YOUR ENEMIES.* Josh sat in a chair with his head down. His eyes were heavy and he was fighting his tears. His mom may have been a drug addict but she was still a woman who he had loved. She was his mom and their bond was unbreakable; despite their disagreements about her drug use and his drug distribution.

Braheem put his arms around his friend and tried to console him.

The Medical Examiner told Josh that unfortunately it appeared his mother had been raped. They took a DNA sample of the semen and put in on file. Josh and Braheem both were disgusted. They knew the only two people responsible for this act were Willie and Sanchez.

After Josh signed the necessary paperwork, he and Braheem left out the building and got into Braheem's Navigator. As they pulled out of the parking lot, Braheem's cell phone started ringing.

'Hello," he said. "Braheem, one of my eyes and ears just came through big time," Edna said. "Me and Josh on our way over there now," Braheem said. "No, meet me at our stash house on 42nd and Westminster Avenue," Edna said. "Cool, I'm on my way now," Braheem said. "How is Josh doing," Edna asked sincerely. "Hold on," Braheem said, passing Josh the phone.

"Edna, what's up," Josh said, wiping his tears away. "Was it her," Edna asked. "Yeah, it was my mom," Josh said sadly. "I'm sorry, Josh," Edna said, wishing the outcome would have been different. "Them niggas raped her before they killed her," Josh said, as he felt the rage boiling in his blood.

"What, they raped her though," Edna said. "Yes, they raped my mom," Josh cried. "Josh calm down. You'll have your chance for revenge very shortly. One of the snakes has finally come out of hiding," Edna said. Her words quickly calmed Josh down. Now he was focused on what he was going to do to the bastards that killed and raped his mom.

"I'll see y'all soon. Alright bye," Edna said, ending the call.

Edna looked over at Coffe and said, "Go get Mr. Big. I'm gonna need him for somebody!"

Coffe quickly got off the sofa and came back into the living room with Mr. Big inside of her hands. Edna took Mr. Big from out of Coffe's hands and put him inside of a black backpack.

"Don't go nowhere and don't answer the phone unless it's me calling," Edna said, as she put on her jacket. After a short kiss, Coffe watched Edna rush out of the front door and get inside of her car and speed off.

Inside Shanika's House...

Sanchez was lying on the bed while Shanika's naked body was mounted on top of his. Shanika rode his dick like no other and gave Sanchez the thrill he had been longing.

"Yeah, Papi, you like this pussy don't you! Come for me again! Come on, Papi!! Yes, Yes, Your Big Dick feels so good inside my wet pussy! Come on, Papi, make this pussy wetter," Shanika screamed out.

Sanchez was laid out on the bed, as Shanika fucked him non-stop. Her pussy was juiced up and she had the best fuck-game he had ever known. Whore or not, he enjoyed being with Shanika. He had already cum twice, and now that she was riding him he was ready to buss again.

Shanika had Sanchez's arms pinned down and she was aggressive and fully in control. Shanika was dominant and his hard dick didn't stand a chance once she her pussy started to pulsate and pull his dick in closer for the kill.

Shanika made sure Sanchez got the best fuck in his entire life because her reward money was on the line.

"I miss this Big Fat Dick!! I love it Papi... Cum in this good wet pussy," Shanika moaned out. "Shit, I can't hold on no more...Damn, I'm cuming again," Sanchez yelled, as another orgasm swept through his body.

Shanika felt his legs trembling beneath her and she knew it was because of the power of her good pussy. When she got up off of Sanchez's sagging dick, she looked down at his exhausted, sweaty naked body; she knew she had him.

"I'll be right back, Papi. Let me go check on my kids," Shanika said. Sanchez heard her but he was too tired to respond. When Shanika walked out the bedroom and closed the door, she ran to the phone and called Edna. After she hung up with her she walked back into her bedroom and smiled as she saw Sanchez sleeping peacefully on the bed.

As his snores filled the air all she could think about was the money she would have. She didn't give a damn about what would happen to Sanchez.

Chapter Fifty-Nine
A ROSE AMONG THORNS II

Downtown Philadelphia...

Inside his lawyer's large conference room, Eric stood up and shook everyone's hand. The deal for his five new properties was finally done. It had cost Eric close to five hundred thousand dollars but it was money well spent. After everyone had left out of the room, Eric and his lawyer, Steven, sat back down and lit up two Cuban cigars.

"How's Rose," Steven asked. "She's doing fine. After I leave here I'm going by to see her," Eric said, blowing a cloud of smoke into the air. "You did a great job, Steve. I like the whole take this offer of the whole deal is a dude thing you did. Great way to bogard a deal," Eric said smilingly.

"Hey, that's what I get paid for," Steve said. "True. I need another big favor from you," Eric said. "Anything. You name it," Steve said confidently. "I have a duffle bag in my trunk with five hundred thousand dollars cash. I need you to clean it up and pay our sellers with that," Eric said, as Steve looked at him and smiled.

"Not a problem. They'll have their checks promptly," he said.

Presbyterian Hospital...

"I told you Joyce that everything would turn out right," Rose said, looking into Joyce's watery eyes. Rose reached out and grabbed Joyce's hand. "I told you that the circle of eternal love can never be broken. You and Braheem are soul mates. Y'all relationship has already been written in God's book of love," Rose said.

"I prayed so hard, Rose" Joyce cried.
"Just keep praying, Joyce because the devil never takes a second, minute, hour or day off," Rose said. "And always remember your man is your King. Treat him like that always and he won't go nowhere," Rose continued.

"Don't worry, I ain't gonna make the same mistake twice. He will always know that he has a queen by his side to the end of time," Joyce said, as they reached out and gave each other a long, sisterly hug.

Inside Shanika's House...

While Sanchez slept on top of the bed, he never saw the tall, dark-skinned man remove his gun from off the nightstand. Shanika and her kids were all sitting inside of the back bedroom. She was told to go there and wait. Two men stood over Sanchez's naked body and when he opened his eyes, he thought he was seeing things. He wasn't. The handle from the .357 Magnum knocked Sanchez out cold. Another hard blow to his head was to ensure he would stay out long enough to get his nude body tied up with silver duct tape.

After Sanchez was all tied up, they wrapped his body in a blanket and picked him up; and then they carried his body downstairs and out of the door. When Shanika heard them leaving, she opened the bedroom door and rushed out of the room. She quickly ran over to the window and watched as they threw Sanchez's wrapped up body into a black Chevy van, and then raced off down the street.

When Shanika walked downstairs into the living room a big smile quickly appeared on her face. On top of the living room coffee table was her reward money. Shanika ran over and picked up the money. She noticed a letter on the table which read, *Keep doing your thing! They don't understand the power of the pussy. And always keep those eyes and ears to the streets! LADY BOSS*

The first person she called was her elderly landlord to tell him that she had the rent money. Shanika gathered up all of her money and walked back upstairs. She looked at her four children and smiled because life was going to be a lot easier for a while.

Chapter Sixty
A ROSE AMONG THORNS II

**Inside Braheem's
West Philly Stash House...**

After Sanchez had finally opened up his dazed and confused eyes, the first thing he noticed was he was no longer at Shanika's. His naked body was tied down to a bed. Standing in front of Sanchez was Edna, Josh and Braheem; each holding a loaded gun in their hands. Edna abruptly snatched the silver duct tape from over his mouth.

"I knew one day pussy would get you in trouble. And right now, Sanchez, you're in real big trouble," Edna said. "Fuck you bitch! Kill me, I ain't scared to die," Sanchez barked. "Willie is gonna kill all y'all muthafuckas!!! Just wait and see," Sanchez shouted.

Braheem walked over to Sanchez and looked into his eyes. "Sanchez, I'm sorry to have to tell you this because it fucks up your plans, but Willie will be dead before tomorrow morning."
"Never! Y'all will never get me to tell you where Willie is at, Never," Sanchez yelled. "We don't need you to tell us you stupid son-of-a-bitch! Our friend, Shanika, yeah her, she got the address from the cab driver who picked you up from Willie's place," Braheem said, taking the small piece of paper from out of his pocket.

"44th and Samson Street," Braheem smiled.

"Fuck you! Fuck all y'all," Sanchez shouted as he tried to free himself from the tight ropes that held him down to the bed. "Kill me now pussy," Sanchez said. "In time," Edna said.

"Why did you do it," Josh asked.
"Do what, nigga... Oh, yeah, fuck your mom before I blew her fucking brains out," Sanchez laughed. "Man, that crack head had some good pussy too," Sanchez laughed out loud.

Josh aimed his 9mm at Sanchez's head but before he could squeeze, Edna knocked his arm away. "No, Josh, I need you and Braheem for a minute. I have a great idea," she smiled.

Braheem and Josh followed Edna out of the room, leaving Sanchez inside the room alone. A few moments later Edna walked back into the room by herself. But this time she was carrying her black backpack in her hand. Edna stood in front of Sanchez and started to undress.

"Bitch, what the fuck is you doing," Sanchez said, looking confused. "You raped my friend's mother and now I'm gonna show you what it feels like for someone to rape you," Edna said, taking off all her clothes except for her bra and panties.

"Bitch, what the fuck are you talking about? Just kill me and get it over with," Sanchez yelled. "No, that would be too easy," Edna said, unzipping her backpack and taking out her 10" strap-on dildo; whom she nicknamed Mr. Big.

"What the fuck you gonna do with that," Sanchez shouted. "Tear you a new asshole, mother fucker!!!" Edna walked behind Sanchez body. His legs were already spread apart and he was firmly tied down. Edna strapped up and then she reached into the backpack and took out a small jar of Vaseline. She rubbed it all over Mr. Big.

"Bitch!! !YOU NASTY BITCH! !! I'm a fuckin man," he yelled out. "No, men don't rape women. You're a coward," Edna said, as she climbed on top of Sanchez's naked body and forcefully slid the 10" Mr. Big into Sanchez's virgin asshole.

"SHIT BITCH STOOOOOOOPPPPPP!!!!" Sanchez screamed out, as Edna forced the entire dildo inside his ass. Edna stroke was crazy, like she had been born with a dick between her legs instead of a pussy.

"STOOOOOOOPPPPPPPPPP," Sanchez continued to yell out in pain.

"Shut up, bitch," Edna said, slapping him in the face. Edna watched as streaks of blood dripped down from Sanchez's asshole.

"Fuck you, you dirty bitch," Sanchez cried out, as tears of humiliation fell down his face.

"No, nigga, I'm fucking you," Edna said, pounding faster and harder.

Right outside the door, Josh and Braheem stood and could hear everything that was going on inside the bedroom. After thirty-five minutes, Edna was still inside the room going strong. Sanchez had a small pool of blood underneath his body. The outside of his asshole had turned dark red and deep blue.

"You wanna rape women, you coward! How does it feel to get a taste of your own medicine," Edna said, thrusting harder. "Stop, please just stop," Sanchez begged.

"Now you want mercy but you showed my friend's mom none. Pussy, you better be glad I'm tired of smelling your bloody ass," Edna said, as she finally climbed off of Sanchez's body.

Edna walked around and looked into Sanchez's scared, and humiliated face. She took off her 10" dildo and threw Mr. Big to the floor. After she put back on her clothes, Edna walked over and looked into Sanchez's eyes.

"When you meet the devil, please tell him that that bitch Lady Boss fucked your life all up," she said. Edna grabbed her dildo and Vaseline and then put them back inside her backpack. Then she walked out of the bedroom.

Moments later Josh walked into the room with his loaded pistol. Sanchez looked at Josh but did not say a word. He knew that words were no longer needed. He had begged for death and now the grim reaper was upon him. When Josh squeezed the trigger of his 9mm, he emptied the entire clip into Sanchez head and body.

After Braheem and Edna walked outside, she passed Braheem Sanchez's keys to the apartment he had been sharing with Willie.

"I got somebody over there working things out for me. When Willie leaves, you can go in and do your thing. I'll be close by," Edna said, walking over to her car and driving off. Once Josh got inside of Braheem's truck they sped off behind her.

Chapter Sixty-One
A ROSE AMONG THORNS II

Later That Night
44th & Samson Street...

Willie had called Sanchez's cell phone seven times without getting an answer. He left Sanchez five voice mails and was waiting for a return call. His intuition told him that something was wrong. Willie walked over to the window and cautiously looked outside. Everything on the small, quiet street seemed to be okay. Willie grabbed his 9mm and put on his black leather jacket, but before he left out the apartment he called Sanchez's cell phone one more time. Still, there was no answer.

Willie walked out of the front door and quickly got into his truck. His mind was racing with thoughts of uncertainty. Tonight Willie and Sanchez had planned on shooting up Braheem's major drug house. Willie needed Sanchez to shoot the AK-47 while he drove the car. Now Sanchez was nowhere to be found.

He started his car and pulled off down the dark street. As he sped off into the darkness of the night, Willie never noticed the three sets of eyes that had been watching his every move. Edna was inside a tan Toyota Camry parked at the end of the block, while Braheem and Josh were inside of a dark green Mazda 929; laying low behind the guard of the tinted windows. Braheem had parked his truck just a few blocks away, next to Edna's Maxima.

Twenty minutes after Willie had left his apartment, he pulled his truck up in front of Shanika's house. He beeped his horn until she came to the window and stuck her head out.

"Damn, I heard you! My kids is sleeping. What's up," she said angrily. "Is Sanchez up there," Willie said. "You just missed him about five minutes ago," Shanika said. "He lost his cell phone inside the cab that brought him here," she said, lying through her teeth.

"Oh, that's why he ain't call me or answer my calls," Willie said." Yeah, but he ain't here now and my kids is all sleep. He should be on his way home or there by now. Alright, I have to go" Shanika said, closing the window.

Shanika peeped out the window and watched Willie speed off down the street. She sat back on her bed and smiled. Edna had called and informed her that Willie would probably be there to see what's up with Sanchez. She told Shanika exactly what to say when he showed up at her house, and Shanika did exactly what she was told.

Willie was now finally feeling relieved. He quickly navigated his truck through traffic and hurried back to his apartment. He was happy to know that his intuition was off and that his young thug, Sanchez, was alright and probably waiting for him to come back to the apartment.

When Willie pulled up in front of the apartment, he noticed the light in Sanchez's room was turned on. It was just the confirmation he needed. After Willie got out of the truck he rushed inside.

"Sanchez, Yo Sanchez," Willie called out as he entered the apartment. He walked towards Sanchez's bedroom and opened the door.

"Yo, Sanchez," Willie said. He began to freeze as he noticed the 9mm that Braheem had pointed at his head.

"What's up, Willie? Long time no see," Braheem said. When Willie turned around, Edna and Josh were standing behind him with their guns drawn.

"Ahh, shit," Willie mumbled to himself. Josh quickly pushed Willie to the floor. When his gun fell out from under his shirt, Edna stepped on it and immediately picked it up. Willie knew he had been set up.

"Sanchez gave me up, huh," he said. "No, the cab company did, stupid," Braheem said. "And my good friend, Shanika, she played a part in this too," Edna laughed. "That stinking bitch! I told Sanchez she wasn't no good," Willie said, angrily banging his fist on the floor.

"Where's Sanchez," Willie said, already knowing the answer once his words escaped from his mouth. "Your young, dumb flunky got fucked over pretty bad," Edna said, laughing at the irony of it all. "He won't be around to kill no more kids or rape no more women," Edna continued.

"Willie, Willie, Willie," Braheem said, looking at Willie's terrified face. "Your greed for money has put you in a real fucked up position. You started a war you couldn't win and now so many lives have been lost because of one man's greed. Everybody in your crew is dead and gone and it's all because of you, Willie." Braheem said.

As he stood over Willie's body he continued, "I'm through talking, Willie. I have a date with my woman tonight. So let's just get to the Goodbye,"

Braheem fired three quick, silent shots into Willie's head. Willie's body sunk into the floor and his blood began to drain from his wounds. Braheem stood back and shot Willie two more times in his neck just to make sure he was dead. Since they were wearing gloves they didn't have to worry about wiping the place down, so they made a swift exit out of the apartment.

Two days later the police discovered Willie's corpse inside the apartment. That same day, Sanchez's mangled, sodomized corpse was found in Fairmount Park, just a few feet away from where Gayle's body was discovered. The Philadelphia homicide unit had no clues or witnesses to help them with either case. And after they checked both men's criminal records, they were actually relieved to have two young maniacs off the street.

Willie and Sanchez names were added to the long list of unsolved homicides in Philadelphia; the same list that they had put so many others names on. Karma had come to collect her debt and just as the saying goes, "What goes around, comes around."

Chapter Sixty-Two
A ROSE AMONG THORNS II

Three Weeks Later
North Philly...

Jose was seated in a leather chair looking at the three people who stood in front of him.
"So this is what you want to do, Braheem," Jose asked. "Yeah, I'm positive, Jose. Here's what I owe you and it's not a penny short," Braheem said, walking over and placing the large green duffle bag by Jose's leg.

"And Eric, my good friend, what do you think of all this," Jose said, lighting up his Cuban cigar. "I think it's a win-win situation. It's time to pass the torch once again and Lady Boss is the one to get it next. I give you my word, Jose, she will live by the same code that me and Braheem lived by. The code of loyalty," Eric said.

Jose stood up from his chair. He looked at all the stern faces that stood around him, his three bodyguards and the three young people who stood in front of him. Jose blew a thick cloud of smoke into the air and then he walked over to Braheem and shook his hand.

"Braheem, you are free to go. Eric, keep him straight," Jose said. "Oh, don't worry, I will," Eric smiled. Jose walked up to Eric and looked into his young friend's eyes.

"I'm taking your word, Eric. I hope you're right once again," he said, shaking Eric's hand. "Like I told you, Jose, you won't be disappointed," Eric said, confidently.

Jose blew another cloud of smoke in the air and finally walked up to Edna.

"So they call you Lady Boss, huh," he said as a small grin came to his face. "Yeah, Eric gave me the name," Edna said, with nothing but business written all over her face. "And why's that," Jose asked curiously. "Because I know how to control situations and people. I am what I am and that's a boss. I'll die by the code of loyalty and my principals don't change for no man or woman," Edna said.

Jose shook his head in agreement and smiled. "So do you think you can run this whole city," Jose said. Edna looked straight into Jose's eyes and said, "No disrespect but anything a man can do, a woman can do better."

Jose walked back to his chair and sat down. For a few moments everyone in the room was silent. The smoke from his cigar lingered in the air.

"Okay, Lady Boss, your first shipment of five hundred kilos will be waiting for you tomorrow. Someone will call you with all the instructions. Good luck…you only get one chance. Don't fuck this up."

Eric, Braheem and Edna all walked out of the door. This was what Edna had wanted and her hand could stand it. She knew she would always have Eric's and Braheem's help if she ever needed it; but she was now the Boss.

Chapter Sixty-Three
A ROSE AMONG THORNS II

Ten Months Later
July 4th ...

Inside St. Mary's Baptist Church, Eric and Rose stood face to face as the short, elderly preacher read each other their marital vows. Eric's best man, Braheem, stood right by his side and Joyce, the very happy maid of honor was standing tall by the bride to be.

Eric was handsomely dressed in an all-white tailor made tuxedo with a pair of white Muri alligator shoes, and Rose had on her beautiful, elegant and form fitting white wedding dress; that had a twelve foot long train floating behind her.

The church was crowded and many people had tears of joy falling from their eyes. The couple was overjoyed and thankful to be in the church exchanging their vows. Eric looked at Rose's plumped round stomach and smiled. Rose was five months pregnant with their first child and both couldn't be happier.

Edna and Coffe sat next to each other; both overjoyed and happy to finally see the lovebirds make it official. Levi stood up next to Josh, holding on to his shoulder for support. Joyce's mother sat in the front row, holding her beautiful newborn granddaughter. The baby's name was Braheema, named after her father of course. Joyce's two younger sisters, Brandy and Aiesha, were the flower girls.

Rose glanced over at all the smiling family and friends and she couldn't believe it. This was the happiest day of her life. Rose had come a long way and this moment had felt surreal. She had survived the projects and an attack on her life; and now she would be able to marry the man of her dreams. She gave God all the glory and was thankful that she had always kept her faith.

As the tears began to slide down her face, Rose looked over at her father, who was also shedding tears of joy, and she smiled at him.

Just three weeks earlier, Johnny Ray's life sentence was vacated by the Third Circuit Court of Appeals, and now he was present to give his daughter away. He was always Rose's rock and she was always his. Johnny Ray smiled back at his daughter and then he put his arms around his crying wife.

Rose turned and faced Eric. Her King was ready to make her his Queen.

"With the powers invested in me, I now pronounce you husband and wife. You may now kiss your bride," the preacher said.

Eric wrapped his arms around his beautiful pregnant wife and they shared an intimate and intense kiss. Cheers and whistles erupted from the large crowd of family and friends. After Eric and his lovely new wife had finished kissing, they walked hand in hand down the aisle.

Johnny Ray approached his new son-in-law and hugged him. Then he reached out and hugged his beautiful pregnant daughter. He then whispered into

Rose's ear, "Remember, never be anything less than a Queen."

THE BEGINNING,
because there is no END
to true LOVE.

"Who can find a virtuous wife? For her worth is far above rubies. The heart of her husband safely Trust her; so he will have no lack of gain. She does him good and not evil all the days of her life. -Proverbs 31:10-12

"Love is not the person you can see yourself with.
Love is the person you cannot see yourself without." -

Available Friday, November 29th, 2013!!!

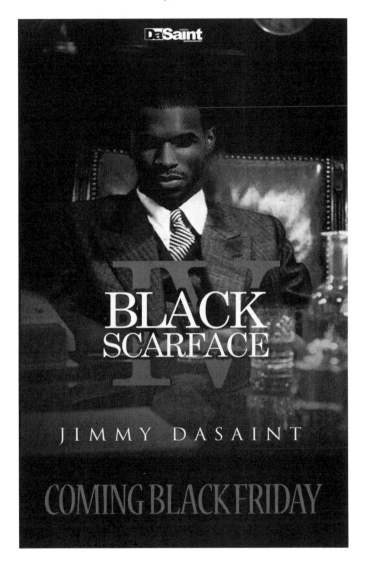

30696855R00119

Made in the USA
Lexington, KY
15 March 2014